FRANCES OF THE RANGES

FRANCES PULLED BACK ON MOLLY'S BRIDLE REINS.

Frontispiece (Page 125).

FRANCES OF THE RANGES

OR

THE OLD RANCHMAN'S TREASURE

BY

AMY BELL MARLOWE

AUTHOR OF
THE OLDEST OF FOUR, THE GIRLS OF HILLCREST
FARM, WYN'S CAMPING DAYS, ETC.

Illustrated

NEW YORK
GROSSET & DUNLAP
PUBLISHERS

Made in the United States of America

CONTENTS

v

vi CONTENTS

FRANCES OF THE RANGES

CHAPTER I

THE ADVENTURE IN THE COULIE

THE report of a bird gun made the single rider in sight upon the short-grassed plain pull in her pinto and gaze westerly toward the setting sun, now going down in a field of golden glory.

The pinto stood like a statue, and its rider seemed a part of the steed, so well did she sit in her saddle. She gazed steadily under her hand—gazed and listened.

Finally, she murmured: " That's the snarl of a lion—sure. Get up, Molly! "

The pinto sprang forward. There was a deep coulie ahead, with a low range of grass-covered hills beyond. Through those hills the lions often came down onto the grazing plains. It was behind these hills that the sun was going down, for the hour was early.

As she rode, the girl loosened the gun she carried in the holster slung at her hip. On her saddle horn was coiled a hair rope.

She was dressed in olive green—her blouse, open at the throat, divided skirts, leggings, and broad-brimmed hat of one hue. Two thick plaits of sunburned brown hair hung over her shoulders, and to her waist. Her grey eyes were keen and rather solemn. Although the girl on the pinto could not have been far from sixteen, her face seemed to express a serious mind.

The scream of that bane of the cattlemen—the mountain lion—rang out from the coulie again. The girl clapped her tiny spurs against the pinto's flanks, and that little animal doubled her pace. In a minute they were at the head of the slope and the girl could see down into the coulie, where low mesquite shrubs masked the bottom and the little spring that bubbled there.

Something was going on down in the coulie. The bushes waved; something rose and fell in their midst like a flail. There was a voice other than that of the raucous tones of the lion, and which squalled almost as loudly!

A little to one side of the shrubs stood a quivering grey pony, its ears pointed toward the rumpus in the shrubs, blowing and snorting. The rider of that empty saddle was plainly in trouble with the snarling lion.

The cattlemen of the Panhandle looked upon the lion as they did upon the coyote—save that the former did more damage to the herds. Roping the lion, or shooting it with the pistol, was a general sport. But caught in a corner, the beast—unlike the coyote—would fight desperately. Whoever had attacked this one had taken on a larger contract than he could handle. That was plain.

Urged by the girl the pinto went down the slope of the hollow on a keen run. At the bottom she snorted and swerved from the mesquite clump. The smell of the lion was strong in Molly's nostrils.

" Stand still, Molly! " commanded the girl, and was out of the saddle with an ease that seemed phenomenal. She ran straight toward the thrashing bushes, pistol in hand.

The lion leaped, and the person who had been beating it off with the shotgun was borne down under the attack. Once those sabre-sharp claws got to work, the victim of the lion's charge would be viciously torn.

The girl saw the gun fly out of his hands. The lion was too close upon its prey for her to use the pistol. She slipped the weapon back into its holster and picked up the shotgun. Plunging through the bushes she swung the gun and knocked the beast aside from its prey. The blow showed the power in her young arms and shoulders. The lion rolled over and over, half stunned.

" Quick!" she advised the victim of the lion's attack. " He'll be back at us."

Indeed, scarcely had she spoken when the brute scrambled to its feet. The girl shouldered the gun and pulled the other trigger as the beast leaped.

There was no report. Either there was no shell in that barrel, or something had fouled the trigger. The lion, all four paws spread, and each claw displayed, sailed through the air like a bat, or a flying squirrel. Its jaws were wide open, its teeth bared, and the screech it emitted was, in truth, a terrifying sound.

The girl realized that the original victim of the lion's attack was scrambling to his feet. She dropped to her knee and kept the muzzle of the gun pointed directly for the beast's breast. The empty gun was her only defense in that perilous moment.

" Grab my gun! Here in the holster!" she panted.

The lion struck against the muzzle of the shotgun, and the girl—in spite of the braced position she had taken—was thrown backward to the ground. As she fell the pistol was drawn from its holster.

The empty shotgun had saved her from coming into the embrace of the angry lion, for while she fell one way, the animal went another.   Then came three shots in rapid succession.

She scrambled to her feet, half laughing, and dusting the palms of her gantlets.   The lion was lying a dozen yards away, while the victim of its attack stood near, the blue smoke curling from the revolver.

"My goodness!"

After the excitement was all over that exclamation from the girl seemed unnecessary. But the fact that startled her was, that it was not a man at all to whose aid she had come. He was a youth little older than herself.

"I say!" this young man exclaimed. "That was plucky of you, Miss—awfully plucky, don't you know! That creature would have torn me badly in another minute."

The girl nodded, but seemed suddenly dumb. She was watching the youth keenly from under the longest, silkiest lashes, it seemed to Pratt Sanderson, he had ever seen.

"I hope you're not hurt?" he said, shyly, extending the pistol toward the girl. She stood with her hands upon her hips, panting a little, and with plenty of color in her brown cheeks.

"How about you?" she asked, shortly.

It was true the young man appeared much the worse for the encounter. In the first place, he stood upon one foot, a good deal like a crane, for his left ankle had twisted when he fell. His left arm, too, was wrenched, and he felt a tingling sensation all through the member, from the shoulder to the tips of his fingers.

Beside, his sleeve was ripped its entire length, and the lion's claws had cut deep into his arm. The breast of his shirt was in strips.

"I say! I'm hurt, worse than I thought, eh?" he said, a little uncertainly. He wavered a moment on his sound foot, and then sank slowly to the grass.

"Wait! Don't let yourself go!" exclaimed the girl, getting into quick action. "It isn't so bad."

She ran for the leather water-bottle that hung from her saddle. Molly had stood through the trouble without moving. Now the girl filled the bottle at the spring.

Pratt Sanderson was lying back on his elbows, and the white lids were lowered over his black eyes.

The treatment the range girl gave him was rather rough, but extremely efficacious. She dashed half the contents of the bottle into his face, and he sat up, gasping and choking. She tore away his tattered shirt in a most matter-of-fact manner and began to bathe the scratches on his chest with her kerchief (quickly unknotted from

around her throat), which she had saturated with
water.   Fortunately, the wounds were not very
deep, after all.

"You—you must think me a silly sort of
chap," he gasped.   "Foolish to keel over like
this—— "

"You haven't been used to seeing blood," the
girl observed.   "That makes a difference.   I've
been binding up the boys' cuts and bruises all my
life.   Never was such a place as the old Bar-T for
folks getting hurt."

"Bar-T?" ejaculated the young man, with sudden interest.   "Then you must be Miss Rugley,
Captain Dan Rugley's daughter?"

"Yes, sir," said the girl, quietly.   "Captain
Rugley is my father."

"And you're going to put on that very clever
spectacle at the Jackleg schoolhouse next month?
I've heard all about it—and what you have done
toward making it what Bill Edwards calls a howl-
ing success.   I'm stopping with Bill.   Mrs.
Edwards is my mother's friend, and I'm the
advance guard of a lot of Amarillo people who
are coming out to the Edwardses just to see your
'Pageant of the Panhandle.'   Bill and his wife
are no end enthusiastic about it."

The deeper color had gradually faded out of
the girl's cheeks.   She was cool enough now; but

she kept her eyes lowered, just the same. He would have liked to see their expression once more. There had been a startled look in their grey depths when first she glanced at him.

"I am afraid they make too much of my part in the affair," said she, quietly. "I am only one of the committee—— "

"But they say you wrote it all," the young fellow interposed, eagerly.

"Oh—*that!* It happened to be easy for me to do so. I have always been deeply interested in the Panhandle—'The Great American Desert' as the old geographies used to call all this great Middle West, of Kansas, Nebraska, the Indian Territory, and Upper Texas.

"My father crossed it among the first white men from the Eastern States. He came back here to settle—long before I was born, of course— when a plow had never been sunk in these range lands. He belongs to the old cattle régime. He wouldn't hear until lately of putting wheat into any of the Bar-T acres."

"Ah, well, by all accounts he is one of the few men who still know how to make money out of cows," laughed Pratt Sanderson. "Thank you, Miss Rugley. I can't let you do anything more for me—— "

"You are a long way from the Edwards'

place," she said. " You'd better ride to the Bar-T
for the night. We will send a boy over there with
a message, if you think Mrs. Edwards will be
worried."

" I suppose I'd better do as you say," he said,
rather ruefully. " Mrs. Edwards *will* be worried
about my absence over supper time. She says I'm
such a tenderfoot."

For a moment a twinkle came into the veiled
grey eyes; the new expression illumined the girl's
face like a flash of sunlight across the shadowed
field.

" You rather back up her opinion when you
tackle a lion with nothing but birdshot—and one
barrel of your gun fouled in the bargain," she
said. " Don't you think so? "

" But I killed it with a revolver! " exclaimed
the young fellow, struggling to his feet again.

" That pistol throws a good-sized bullet," said
the ranchman's daughter, smiling. " But I'd never
think of picking a quarrel with a lion unless I had
a good rope, or something that threw heavier lead
than birdshot."

He looked at her, standing there in the after-
glow of the sunset, with honest admiration in his
eyes.

" I *am* a tenderfoot, I guess," he admitted.
" And you were not scared for a single moment! "

"Oh, yes, I was," and Frances Rugley's laugh was low and musical. "But it was all over so quickly that the scare didn't have a chance to show. Come on! I'll catch your pony, and we'll make the Bar-T before supper time."

CHAPTER II

THE grey was a well-trained cow-pony, for the Edwards' ranch was one of the latest in that section of the Panhandle to change from cattle to wheat raising. A part of its range had not as yet been plowed, and Bill Edwards still had a corral full of good riding stock.

Pratt Sanderson got into his saddle without much trouble and the girl whistled for Molly.

" I'll throw that lion over my saddle," she said. " Molly won't mind it much—especially if you hold her bridle with her head up-wind."

" All right, Miss Rugley," the young man returned. " My name is Pratt Sanderson—I don't know that you know it."

" Very well, Mr. Sanderson," she repeated.

" They don't call me *that* much," the young fellow blurted out. " I answer easier to my first name, you know—Pratt."

" Very well, Pratt," said the girl, frankly. " I am Frances Rugley—Frances Durham Rugley."

She lifted the heavy lion easily, flung it across Molly, and lashed it to the saddle; then she

11

mounted in a hurry and the ponies started for the
ranch trail which Frances had been following
before she heard the report of the shotgun.

The youth watched her narrowly as they rode
along through the dropping darkness. She was a
well-matured girl for her age, not too tall, her
limbs rounded, but without an ounce of superfluous
flesh. Perhaps she knew of his scrutiny; but her
face remained calm and she did not return his
gaze. They talked of inconsequential things as
they rode along.

Pratt Sanderson thought: " *What* a girl she is!
Mrs. Edwards is right—she's the finest specimen
of girlhood on the range, bar none! And she is
more than a little intelligent—quite literary, don't
you know, if what they say is true of her. Where
did *she* learn to plan pageants? Not in one of
these schoolhouses on the ranges, I bet an apple!
And she's a cowgirl, too. Rides like a female
Centaur; shoots, of course, and throws a rope.
Bet she knows the whole trade of cattle herding.

" Yet there isn't a girl who went to school with
me at the Amarillo High who looks so well-bred,
or who is so sure of herself and so easy to converse
with."

For her part, Frances was thinking: " And he
doesn't remember a thing about me! Of course,
he was a senior when I was in the junior class. He

ıas already forgotten most of his schoolmates, I
ıuppose.

"But that night of Cora Grimshaw's party he
lanced with me six times. He was in the bank
:hen, and had forgotten all 'us kids,' I suppose.
Funny how suddenly a boy grows up when he gets
)ut of school and into business. But me——

"Well! I should have known him if we hadn't
net for twenty years. Perhaps that's because he
s the first boy I ever danced with—in town, I
nean. The boys on the ranch don't count."

Her tranquil face and manner had not betrayed
—nor did they betray now—any of her thoughts
ıbout this young fellow whom she remembered
ıo clearly, but who plainly had not taxed his mem-
)ry with her.

That was the way of Frances Durham Rugley.
A great deal went on in her mind of which nobody
—not even Captain Dan Rugley, her father—
lreamed.

Left motherless at an early age, the ranchman's
laughter had grown to her sixteenth year differ-
:nt from most girls. Even different from most
)ther girls of the plains and ranges.

For ten years there was not a woman's face—
vhite, black, or red—on the Bar-T acres. The
Captain had married late in life, and had loved
Frances' mother devotedly. When she died sud-

denly the man could not bear to hear or see another woman on the place.

Then Frances grew into his heart and life, and although the old wound opened as the ranchman saw his daughter expand, her love and companionship was like a healing balm poured into his sore heart.

The man's strong, fierce nature suddenly went out to his child and she became all and all to him—just as her mother had been during the few years she had been spared to him.

So the girl's schooling was cut short—and Frances loved books and the training she had received at the Amarillo schools. She would have loved to go on—to pass her examinations for college preparation, and finally get her diploma and an A. B., at least, from some college.

That, however, was not to be. Old Captain Rugley lavished money on her like rain, when she would let him. She used some of the money to buy books and a piano and pay for a teacher for the latter to come to the ranch, while she spent much midnight oil studying the books by herself.

Captain Rugley's health was not all it should have been. Frances could not now leave him for long.

Until recently the old ranchman had borne lightly his seventy years. But rheumatism had taken hold upon him and he did not stand as straight as of old, nor ride so well.

He was far from an invalid; but Frances realized—more than he did, perhaps—that he had finished his scriptural span of life, and that his present years were borrowed from that hardest of taskmasters, Father Time.

Often it was Frances who rode the ranges, instead of Captain Rugley, viewing the different herds, receiving the reports of underforemen and wranglers, settling disputes between the punchers themselves, looking over chuck outfits, buying hay, overseeing brandings, and helping cut out fat steers for the market trail.

There was nothing Frances of the ranges did not know about the cattle-raising business. And she was giving some attention to the new grain-raising ideas that had come into the Panhandle with the return of the first-beaten farming horde.

For the Texas Panhandle has had its two farming booms. The first advance of the farmers into the ranges twenty-five years or more before had been a rank failure.

"They came here and plowed up little spots in our parsters that air eyesores now," one old cowman said, " and then beat it back East when they found it didn't rain 'cordin' ter schedule. This land ain't good for nothin' 'cept cows."

But this had been in the days of the old un-
fenced ranges, and before dry-farming had
become a science. Now the few remaining cattlemen kept their pastures fenced, and began
to think of raising other feed than river-bottom
hay.

The cohorts of agriculturists were advancing;
the cattlemen were falling back. The ancient
staked plains of the Spanish *conquestadors* were
likely to become waving wheat fields and smiling
orchards.

The young girl and her companion could not
travel fast to the Bar-T ranch-house for two rea-
sons: Pratt Sanderson was sore all over, and the
mountain lion slung across Frances' pony caused
some trouble. The pinto objected to carrying
double—especially when an occasional draft of
evening air brought the smell of the lion to her
nostrils.

The young fellow admired the way in which the
girl handled her mount. He had seen many half-
wild horsemen at the Amarillo street fairs, and
the like; since coming to Bill Edwards' place he
had occasionally observed a good rider handling
a mean cayuse. But this man-handling of a half-
wild pony was nothing like the graceful control
Frances of the ranges had over Molly. The pinto
danced and whirled and snorted, and once almost

got her quivering nose down between her knees—
the first position of the bucking horse.

At every point Frances met her mount with a
stern word, or a firm rein, or a touch of the spur
or quirt, which quickly took the pinto's mind off
her intention of " acting up."

" You are wonderful! " exclaimed the youth,
excitedly. " I wish I could ride half as good as
you do, Miss Frances."

Frances smiled. " You did not begin young
enough," she said. " My father took me in his
arms when I was a week old and rode a half-wild
mustang twenty miles across the ranges to exhibit
me to the man who was our next-door neighbor
in those days. You see, my tuition began early."

It was not yet fully dark, although the ranch-
house lamps were lit, when they came to the home
corral and the big fenced yard in front of the
Bar-T.

Two boys ran out to take the ponies. One of
these Frances instructed to saddle a fresh pony
and ride to the Edwards place with word that
Pratt Sanderson would remain all night at the
Bar-T.

The other boy was instructed to give the mountain lion to one of the men, that the pelt might be
removed and properly stretched for curing.

" Come right in, Pratt," said the girl, with

frank cordiality. " You'll have a chance for a wash and a brush before supper. And dad will find you some clean clothes.

" There's dad on the porch, though he's forbidden the night air unless he puts a coat on. Oh, he's a very, very bad patient, indeed! "

CHAPTER III

THE OLD SPANISH CHEST

PRATT saw a tall, lean man—a man of massive frame, indeed, with a heavy mustache that had once been yellow but had now turned grey, teetering on the rear legs of a hard-bottomed chair, with his shoulders against the wall of the house.

There were plenty of inviting-looking chairs scattered about the veranda. There were rugs, and potted plants, and a lounge-swing, with a big lamp suspended from the ceiling, giving light enough over all.

But the master of the Bar-T had selected a straight-backed, hard-bottomed chair, of a kind that he had been used to for half a century and more. He brought the front legs down with a bang as the girl and youth approached.

"What's kept you, Frances?" he asked, mellowly. "Evening, sir! I take it your health's well?"

He put out a hairy hand into which Pratt confided his own and, the next moment, vowed secretly he would never risk it there again! His left hand tingled badly enough since the attentions of the mountain lion. Now his right felt as though it had been in an ore-crusher.

"This is Pratt Sanderson, from Amarillo," the daughter of the ranchman said first of all. "He's a friend of Mrs. Bill Edwards. He was having trouble with a lion over in Brother's Coulie, when I came along. We got the lion; but Pratt got some scratches. Can't Ming find him a flannel shirt, Dad?"

"Of course," agreed Captain Rugley, his eyes twinkling just as Frances' had a little while before. "You tell him as you go in. Come on, Pratt Sanderson. I'll take a look at your scratches myself."

A shuffle-footed Chinaman brought the shirt to the room Pratt Sanderson had been ushered to by the cordial old ranchman. The Chinaman assisted the youth to get into the garment, too, for Captain Rugley had already swathed the scratches on Pratt's chest and arm with linen, after treating the wounds with a pungent-smelling but soothing salve.

"San Soo, him alle same have dlinner ready sloon," said Ming, sprinkling 'l's' indiscriminately in his information. "Clapen an' Misse Flank wait on pleaza."

The young fellow, when he was presentable, started back for the " pleaza."

Everything he saw—every appointment of the house—showed wealth, and good taste in the use of it. The old ranchman furnished the former, of course; but nobody but Frances, Pratt thought, could have arranged the furnishings and adornments of the house.

The room he was to occupy as a guest was large, square, grey-walled, was hung with bright pictures, a few handsome Navajo blankets, and had heavy soft rugs on the floor. There was a gay drapery in one corner, behind which was a canvas curtain masking a shower bath with nickel fittings.

The water ran off from the shallow marble basin through an open drain under the wall. The bed was of brass and looked comfortable. There was a big steamer chair drawn invitingly near the window which opened into the court, or garden, around which the house was built.

The style of the building was Spanish, or Mexican. A fountain played in the court and there were trees growing there, among the branches of which a few lanterns were lit, like huge fireflies.

In passing back to the front porch of the ranch-house (farther south it would have been called *hacienda*) Pratt noted Spanish and Aztec armor hanging on the walls; high-backed, carven chairs of black oak, mahogany, and other heavy woods; weapons of both modern and ancient Indian manufacture, and those of the style used by Cortez and his cohorts when they marched on the capital city of the great Montezuma.

In a glass-fronted case, too, hung a brilliant cloak of parakeet feathers such as were worn by the Aztec nobles. Lights had been lit in the hall since he had arrived and the treasures were now revealed for the first time to the startled eye of the visitor.

The sight of these things partially prepared him for the change in Frances' appearance. Her smooth brown skin and her veiled eyes were the same. She still wore her hair in girlish plaits. She was quite the simple, unaffected girl of sixteen. But her dress was white, of some soft and filmy material which looked to the young fellow like spider's web in the moonlight. It was cut a little low at the throat; her arms were bared to the elbow. She wore a heavy, glittering belt of alternate red-gold links and green stones, and on one arm a massive, wrought-gold bracelet—a serpent with turquoise eyes.

"Frances is out in her warpaint," chuckled Captain Rugley's mellow voice from the shadow, where he was tipped back in his chair again.

"You gave me these things out of your treasure chest, Daddy, to wear when we had company," said the girl, quite calmly.

She wore the barbarous ornaments with an air of dignity. They seemed to suit her, young as she was. And Pratt knew that the girdle and bracelet must be enormously valuable as well as enormously old.

The expression "treasure chest" was so odd that it stuck in the young man's mind. He was very curious as to what it meant, and determined, when he knew Frances better, to ask about it.

A little silence had fallen after the girl's speech. Then Captain Rugley started forward suddenly and the forelegs of his chair came sharply to the planks.

"Hello!" he said, into the darkness outside the radiance of the porch light. "Who's there?"

Frances fluttered out of her chair. Pratt noted that she slipped into the shadow. Neither she nor the Captain had been sitting in the full radiance of the lamp.

The visitor had heard nothing; but he knew that the old ranchman was leaning forward listening intently.

"Who's there?" the captain demanded again.

"Don't shoot, neighbor!" said a hoarse voice out of the darkness. "I'm jest a-paddin' of it

Amarillo way.   Can I get a flop-down and a bite
here?"

" Only a tramp, Dad," breathed Frances, with
a sigh.

" How did you get into this compound?" demanded Captain Rugley, none the less suspiciously
and sternly.

" I come through an open gate.   It's so 'tarnal
dark, neighbor—— "

" You see those lights down yonder?" snapped
the Captain.   " They are at the bunk-house.
Cook'll give you some chuck and a chance to
spread your blanket.   But don't you let me catch
you around here too long after breakfast to-morrow morning.   We don't encourage hobos, and
we already have all the men hired for the season
we want."

" All right, neighbor," said the voice in the
darkness, cheerfully—too cheerfully, in fact, Pratt
Sanderson thought.   An ordinary man—even one
with the best intentions in the world—would have
been offended by the Captain's brusk words.

A stumbling foot went down the yard.   Captain
Rugley grunted, and might have said something
explanatory, but just then Ming came softly to the
door, whining:

" Dlinner, Misse."

" Guess Pratt's hungry, too," grunted the Cap-

tain, rising. " Let's go in and see what the neighbors have flung over the back fence."

But sad as the joke was, all that Captain Rugley
said seemed so open-hearted and kindly—save
only when he was talking to the unknown tramp—
that the guest could not consider him vulgar.

The dining-room was long, massively furnished,
well lit, and the sideboard exposed some rare
pieces of old-fashioned silver. Two heavy candelabra—the loot of some old cathedral, and of
Spanish manufacture—were set upon either end of
the great serving table.

All these treasures, found in the ranch-house
of a cowman of the Panhandle, astounded the
youth from Amarillo. Nothing Mrs. Bill
Edwards had said of Frances of the ranges and
her father had prepared him for this display.

Captain Rugley saw his eyes wandering from
one thing to the other as Ming served a perfect
soup.

" Just pick-ups over the Border," the old man
explained, with a comprehensive wave of his hand
toward the candelabra and other articles of value.
" I and a partner of mine, when we were in the
Rangers years and years ago, raided over into
Mexico and brought back the bulk of these things.

" We cached them down in Arizona till after I
was married and built this ranch-house. Poor

Lon! Never have heard what became of him. I've got his share of the treasure out of old Don Milo Morales' *hacienda* right here. When he comes for it we'll divide. But I haven't heard from Lon since long before Frances, here, was born."

This was just explanation enough to whet the curiosity of Pratt. Talk of the Texas Rangers, and raiding over the Border, and looting a Mexican *hacienda,* was bound to set the young man's imagination to work.

But the dinner, as it was served in courses, took up Pratt's present attention almost entirely. Never—not even when he took dinner at the home of the president of the bank in Amarillo—had he eaten so well-cooked and well-served a meal.

Despite his commonplace speech, Captain Rugley displayed a familiarity with the niceties of table etiquette that surprised the guest. Frances' mother had come from the East and from a family that had been used to the best for generations. And the old ranchman, in middle age, had set himself the task of learning the niceties of table manners to please her.

He had never fallen back into the old, careless ways after Frances' mother died. He ate to-night in black clothes and a soft, white shirt in the bosom of which was a big diamond. Although he had sat on the veranda without a coat—contrary to his doctor's orders—he had slipped one on when he came to the table and, with his neatly combed hair, freshly shaven face, and well-brushed mustache, looked well groomed indeed.

He would have been a bizarre figure at a city table; nevertheless, he presided at his own board with dignity, and was a splendid foil for the charming figure of Frances opposite.

In the midst of the repast the Captain said, suddenly, to the soft-footed Chinaman:

" Ming! telephone down to Sam at the bunkhouse and see if a hobo has just struck there, on his way to Amarillo. I told him he could get chuck and a sleep. Savvy? "

" Jes so, Clapen," said Ming, softly, and shuffled out.

It was evident that the tramp was on the Captain's mind. Pratt believed there must be some special reason for the old ranchman's worrying over marauders about the Bar-T.

There was nothing to mar the friendliness of the dinner, however; not even when Ming slipped back and said in a low voice to the Captain:

" Him Slilent Slam say no hobo come to blunkhouse."

They finished the meal leisurely; but on rising from the table Captain Rugley removed a heavy

belt and holster from its hook behind the sideboard and slung it about his hips.

Withdrawing the revolver, he spun the cylinder,
made sure that it was filled, and slipped it back in
the holster. All this was done quite as a matter
of course. Frances made no comment, nor did
she seem surprised.

The three went back to the porch for a little
while, although the night air was growing chill.
Frances insisted that her father wear his coat, and
they both sat out of the brighter radiance of the
hanging lamp.

She and her guest were talking about the forthcoming pageant at the Jackleg schoolhouse. Pratt
had begun to feel enthusiastic over it as he learned
more of the particulars.

" People scarcely realize," said Frances, " that
this Panhandle of ours has a history as ancient as
St. Augustine, Florida. And *that*, you know, is
called the oldest white settlement in these United
States.'

" Long, long ago the Spanish explorers, with
Indian guides whom they had enslaved, made a
path through the swarming buffaloes up this way
and called the country *Llano Estacada*, the staked
plain. Our geographers misapplied the name
' Desert ' to this vast country; but Nebraska, Kansas, and Oklahoma threw off that designation

because it was proven that the rains fell more often than was reported."

"What has built up those states," said Pratt, with a smile, " is farming, not cattle."

The Captain grunted, for he had been listening to the conversation.

"You ought to have seen those first hayseeds that tried to turn the ranges into posy beds and wheat fields," he chuckled. "They got all that was coming to them—believe me!"

Frances laughed. "Daddy is still unconverted. He does not believe that the Panhandle is fit for anything but cattle. But he's going to let me have two hundred acres to plow and sow to wheat—he's promised."

The Captain grunted again.

"And last year we grew a hundred acres of milo maize and feterita. Helped on the winter feed—didn't it, Daddy?" and she laughed.

"Got me there, Frances—got me there," admitted the old ranchman. "But I don't hope to live long enough to see the Bar-T raising more wheat than steers."

"No. It's stock-raising we want to follow, I believe," said the girl, calmly. "We must raise feed for our steers, fatten them in fenced pastures, and ship them more quickly."

"My goodness!" exclaimed Pratt, admiringly,

"you talk as though you understood all about it, Miss Frances."

"I think I *do* know something about the new conditions that face us ranchers of the Panhandle," the girl said, quietly. "And why shouldn't I? I have been hearing it talked about, and thinking of it myself, ever since I can remember."

Secretly Pratt thought she must have given her attention to something beside the ranch work and cattle-raising. Of this he was assured when they went inside later, and Frances sat down to the piano. The instrument was in a big room with a bare, polished floor. It was evidently used for dancing. There was a talking machine as well as a piano. The girl played the latter very nicely indeed. There were a few scratches on the floor of the room, and she saw Pratt looking at them.

"I told Ratty M'Gill he shouldn't come in here with the rest of the boys to dance if he didn't take his spurs off," she said. "We have an old-time hoe-down for the boys pretty nearly every week, when we're not too rushed on the ranch. It keeps 'em better contented and away from the towns on pay-days."

"Are the cowpunchers just the same as they used to be?" asked Pratt. "Do they go to town and blow it wide open on pay-nights?"

"Not much. We have a good sheriff. But it

wasn't so long ago that your fancy little city of
Amarillo was nothing but a cattleman's town.
I'm going to have a representation of old Amarillo
in our pageant—you'll see.   It will be true to life,
too, for some of the very people who take part in
our play lived in Amarillo at the time when the
sight of a high hat would draw a fusilade of
bullets from the door of every saloon and dance-
hall."

" Don't! " gasped Pratt.   " Was Amarillo ever
like *that?* "

" And not twenty years ago," laughed Frances.
" It had a few hundred inhabitants—and most of
them ruffians.   Now it claims ten thousand, has
bricked streets that used to be cow trails, electric
lights, a street-car service, and all the comforts and
culture of an ' effete East.' "

Pratt laughed, too.   " It's a mighty comfortable place to live in—beside Bill Edwards' ranch,
for instance.   But I notice here at the Bar-T you
have a great many of the despised Eastern lux-
uries."

" ' Do-funnies ' daddy calls them," said
Frances, smiling.   " Ah! here he is."

The old ranchman came in, the holstered pistol
still slung at his hip.

" All secure for the night, Daddy? " she asked,
looking at him tenderly.

" Locked, barred, and bolted," returned her father. " I tell you, Pratt, we're something of a fort here when we go to bed. The court's free to you; but don't try to get out till Ming opens up in the morning. You see, we're some distance from the bunk-house, and nobody but the two Chinks are here with us now."

" I see, sir," said Pratt.

But he did not see; he wondered. And he wondered more when, after separating from Frances for the night, he found his way through the hall to the door of the room that had been assigned to him for his use.

On the other side of the hall was another door, open more than a crack, with a light shining behind it. Pratt's curiosity got the better of him and he peeped.

Captain Dan Rugley was standing in the middle of the almost bare room, before an old dark, Spanish chest. He had a bunch of keys in one hand and in the other dangled the ancient girdle and the bracelet Frances had worn.

" That must be the ' treasure chest ' she spoke of," thought the youth. " And it looks it! Old, old, wrought-iron work trimmings of Spanish design. What a huge old lock! My! it would take a stick of dynamite to blow that thing open if one hadn't the key."

The Captain moved quickly, turning toward the door. Pratt dodged back—then crept silently away, down the hall.   He did not know that the eye of the old ranchman watched him keenly through the crack of the door.

CHAPTER IV

WHAT HAPPENED IN THE NIGHT

FRANCES looked through her barred window, out over the fenced yard, and down to the few twinkling watch-lights at the men's quarters. All the second-story windows of the ranch-house, overlooking the porch roof, were barred with iron rods set in the cement, like those on the first floor. The Bar-T ranch-house was a veritable fort.

There was a reason for this that the girl did not entirely understand, although her father often hinted at it. His stories of his adventures as a Texas Ranger, and over the Border into Mexico, amused her; but they had not impressed her much. Perhaps, because the Captain always skimmed over the particulars of those desperate adventures which had so spiced his early years—those years before the gentle influence of Frances' mother came into his life.

He had mentioned his partner, " Lon," on this evening. But he seldom particularized about him.

Frances could not remember when her father had gone into Arizona and returned from thence with a wagon-train loaded with many of the most beautiful of their household possessions. It was when she was a very little girl.

With the other things, Captain Rugley had brought back the old Spanish chest which he guarded so anxiously. She did not know what was in the chest—not all its treasures. It was the one secret her father kept from her.

Out of it he brought certain barbarous ornaments that he allowed her to wear now and then. She was as much enamored of jewelry and beautiful adornments as other girls, was Frances of the ranges.

There was perfect trust between her father and herself; but not perfect confidence. No more than Pratt Sanderson, for instance, did she know just how the old ranchman had become possessed of the great store of Indian and Spanish ornaments, or of the old Spanish chest.

Certain she was that he could not have obtained them in a manner to wrong anybody else. He spoke of them as " the loot of old Don Milo Morales' *hacienda*"; but Frances knew well enough that her good father, Captain Dan Rugley, had been no land pirate, no so-called Border ruffian, who had robbed some peaceful Spanish ranch-owner across the Rio Grande of his possessions.

Frances was a bit worried to-night. There were two topics of thought that disturbed her.

Motherless, and with few female friends even, she had been shut away with her own girlish thoughts and fears and wonderings more than most girls of her age. Life was a mystery to her. She lived in books and in romances and in imagination's pictures more than she did in the workaday world about her.

There seems to be little romance attached to the everyday lives we live, no matter how we are situated. The most dreary and uncolored existence, in all probability, there is in the world to-day is the daily life of a real prince or princess. We look longingly over the fence of our desires and consider all sorts and conditions of people outside as happier and far better off than we.

That was the way it was with Frances. Especially on this particular night.

Her unexpected meeting with Pratt Sanderson had brought to her heart and mind more strongly than for months her experiences in Amarillo. She remembered her school days, her school fellows, and the difference between their lives and that which she lived at present.

Probably half the girls she had known at school would be delighted (or thought they would) to change places with Frances of the ranges, right then. But the ranch girl thought how much better off she would be if she were continuing her education under the care of people who could place her in a more cultivated life.

Not that she was disloyal, even in thought, to her father. She loved him intensely—passionately! But the life of the ranges, after her taste of school and association with cultivated people, could not be entirely satisfactory.

So she sat, huddled in a white wool wrapper, by the barred, open window, looking out across the plain. Only for the few lights at the corrals and bunk-house, it seemed a great, horizonless sea of darkness—for there was no moon and a haze had enveloped the high stars since twilight.

No sound came to her ears at first. There is nothing so soundless as night on the plains—unless there be beasts near, either tamed or wild.

No coyote slunk about the ranch-house. The horses were still in the corrals. The cattle were all too far distant to be heard. Not even the song of a sleepy puncher, as he wheeled around the herd, drifted to the barred window of Frances' room.

Her second topic for thought was her father's evident expectation that the ranch-house might be attacked. Every stranger was an object of suspicion to him.

This did not abate one jot his natural Western hospitality. As mark his open-handed reception of Pratt Sanderson on this evening. They kept open house at the Bar-T ranch. But after dark— or, after bedtime at least—the place was barred like a fort in the Indian country!

Captain Rugley never went to his bed save after making the rounds, armed as he had been to-night, with Ming to bolt the doors. The only way a marauder could get into the inner court was by climbing the walls and getting over the roof, and as the latter extended four feet beyond the second-story walls, such a feat was well-nigh impossible.

The cement walls themselves were so thick that they seemed impregnable even to cannon. The roof was of slates. And, as has been pointed out already, all the outer first-floor windows, and all those reached from the porch roof, were barred.

Frances knew that her father had been seriously troubled to-night by the appearance of the strange and unseen tramp in the yard, and the fact that the arrival of that same individual had not been reported from the men's quarters.

Captain Rugley telephoned and learned from his foreman, Silent Sam Harding, that nobody had come to the bunk-house that night asking for lodging and food.

Frances was about to seek her bed. She

yawned, curled her bare toes up closer in the robe, and shivered luxuriously as the night air breathed in upon her. In another moment she would pop in between the blankets and cuddle down——

Something snapped! It was outside, not in!

Frances was wide awake on the instant. Her eyelids that had been so drowsy were propped apart—not by fear, but by excitement.

She had lived a life which had sharpened her physical perceptions to a fine point. She had no trouble in locating the sound that had so startled her. Somebody was climbing the vine at the corner of the veranda roof, not twenty feet from her window. She crouched back, well sheltered in the shadow, but able to see anything that appeared silhouetted between her window and the dark curtain of the night.

There was no light in the room behind her; indeed every lamp in the ranch-house had been extinguished some time before. It was evident that this marauder—whoever he was—had waited for the quietude of sleep to fall upon the place.

Back in the room at the head of Frances' bed hung her belt with the holster pistol she wore when riding about the ranges. In these days it was considered perfectly safe for a girl to ride alone, save that coyotes sometimes came within range, or such a savage creature as had been the introduction of

Pratt Sanderson and herself so recently.   It was
the duty of everybody on the ranges to shoot and
kill these " varmints," if they could.

Frances did not even think of this weapon now.
She did not fear the unknown; only that the mystery of the night, and of his secret pursuit, surrounded him.   Who could he be?   What was he
after?   Should she run to awaken her father, or
wait to observe his appearance above the edge of
the veranda roof?

A dried stick of the vine snapped again.   There
was a squirming figure on the very edge of the
roof.   Frances knew that the unknown lay there,
panting, after his exertions.

CHAPTER V

A DOZEN things she *might* have done afterward appealed to Frances Rugley. But as she crouched by her chamber window watching the squirming human figure on the edge of the roof, she was interested in only one thing:

Who was he?

This question so filled her thought that she was neither fearful nor anxious. Curiosity controlled her actions entirely for the few next minutes. And so she observed the marauder rise up, carefully balance himself on the slates of the veranda roof, and tiptoe away to the corner of the house. He did not come near her window; nor could she see his face. His outlines were barely visible as he drifted into the shadow at the corner—soundless of step now. Only the cracking of the dry branch, as he climbed up, had betrayed him.

"I wish he had come this way," thought Frances. "I might have seen what he looked like. Surely, we have no man on the ranch who would do such a thing. Can it be that father is

41

right?   Did the fellow who hailed us to-night
come here to the Bar-T for some bad purpose? "

She waited several minutes by her window.
Then she bethought her that there was a window
at the end of a cross-hall on the side of the house
where the man had disappeared, out of which she
might catch another glimpse of him.

So she thrust her bare feet into slippers, tied
the robe more firmly about her, and hurried out
of the room.   Nor did she think now of the
charged weapon hanging at the head of her bed.

She believed nobody would be astir in the great
house.   The Chinamen slept at the extreme rear
over the kitchen.   Their guest, Pratt Sanderson,
was on the lower floor and at the opposite side,
with his windows opening upon the court around
which the *hacienda* was built.

Captain Rugley's rooms were below, too.
Frances knew herself to be alone in this part of
the house.

Nothing had ever happened to Frances Rugley
to really terrify her.   Why should she be afraid
now?   She walked swiftly, her robe trailing behind, her slippered feet twinkling in and out under
the nightgown she wore.   In the cross-hall she
almost ran.   There, at the end, was the open window..   Indeed, there were no sashes in these hall
windows at this time of year; only the bars.

The night air breathed in upon her.   Was that
a rustling just outside the bars?   There was no
light behind her and she did not fear being seen
from without.

Tiptoeing, she came to the sill.   Her ears were
quick to distinguish sounds of any character.
There *was* a strange, faint creaking not far from
that wide-open casement.   She could not thrust
her head between the bars now (she remembered
vividly the last time she had done that and got
stuck, and had to shriek for Daddy to come and
help her out), but she could press her face close
against them and stare into the blackness of the
outer world.

There! something stirred.   Her eyes, growing
more accustomed to the darkness, caught the
shadow of something writhing in the air.

What could it be?   Was it alive?   A man,
or——

Then the bulk of it passed higher, and the
strange creaking sound was renewed.   Frances
almost cried aloud!

It was the man she had before seen.   He was
mounting directly into the air.   The over-thrust
of the ranch-house roof made the shadow very
thick against the house-wall.   The man was swinging in the air just beyond this deeper shadow.

" What can he be doing? " Frances thought.

She had almost spoken the question aloud. But she did not want to startle him—not yet.

First, she must learn what he was about. Then she would run and tell her father. This night raider was dangerous—there was no doubt of that.

" Oh! " quavered Frances, suddenly, and under her breath. The uncertain bulk of the man hanging in the air had disappeared!

For a minute she could not understand. He had disappeared like magic. His very corporeal body—and she noted that it had been bulky when she first saw him roll over the edge of the veranda roof and sit up—had melted into thin air.

And then she saw something swinging, pendulum-like, before her. She thrust an arm between the bars and seized the thing. It was a rope ladder.

The whole matter, then, was as plain as daylight. The man had climbed to the porch roof, with the rope ladder wound around his body. That was what had made him seem so bulky.

Selecting this spot as a favorable one, he had flung the grappling-hook over the eaves. There must be some break in the slates which held the hook. Once fastened there, the man had quickly worked his way up to the roof, and Frances had arrived just in time to see him squirm out of sight.

There were a dozen questions in Frances' mind.
How did he get here? Who was he? What did
he want? Was he the man Captain Rugley had
seemed to be expecting to try to make a raid upon
the ranch-house? Was he alone? How did he
know he could make the hook of his ladder.fast
at this point? Was there a traitor about who had
broken a slate in the roof? Or was the broken
place the result of an accident, and the marauder
had noted it by daylight from the ground?

Question after question flashed through her
mind. But there was one query far more important than all the others:

Where was the man going over the roof?

Frances let the ladder swing away from her
clutch again. If she held it the fellow above
might become alarmed.

She turned from the window and darted back
along the hall. At the end was a door leading
out onto the balcony which surrounded the inner
court of the house at the level of the second story.
The roof sloped out from the main wall of the
building at this inner side, just as it did in front—
indeed, the eaves were even longer. But the pil-
lars of the balcony met the overhang at its verge,
making it very easy indeed for an active person
to swarm down from the roof.

Once on the balcony, the interior of the house

was open to a marauder by a dozen doors, while there were likewise two flights of stairs descending directly into the court.

There were no lamps in the court now.   It was a well, filled with grey shadows.   Frances leaned over the balustrade and heard no sound.   She looked up.   The edge of the roof was a sharply defined line against the lighter background of the sky.   But there was no moving figure silhouetted against that background.

Where had the man gone who had climbed the rope ladder?   He could not so quickly have descended into the court; Frances was positive of that.

She shivered a little.   There was something quite disturbing about this mysterious marauder. She wished now she had aroused her father immediately on first descrying the man.

She started around the gallery.   Her father's room lay upon the other side of the house.   She could reach his windows by descending the outside stairway there.   Her slippered feet made no sound; the wool robe did not rustle.   Had she been seen by anybody she might have been taken for a ghost.   But the black shadow of the roof of the gallery swathed Frances about, and it would have taken keen eyes indeed to distinguish her form.

Down the stair she sped.   She was almost at its foot when something held her motionless again. She halted with a gasp, while before her, from the direction of the softly playing fountain, a figure drifted in.

Frances held her breath.   Was *this* the man who had come over the roof of the house?   Or was it another?

She crouched silently behind the railing.   The figure passed her, going toward her father's windows.   She dared not whisper, for she did not think it bulky enough for her father's huge frame.

On the trail of the figure she started, her heart palpitating with excitement, yet never for a moment considering her own peril.

There were other bedrooms beside that of Captain Rugley in this direction.   And there was that small apartment in which the old Spanish chest was so carefully locked.

Captain Rugley never allowed the key of this door or the key of the chest to go out of his possession.   He had always intimated that if a thief ever tried to break into the Bar-T ranch-house, he would first of all try to get at the treasure chest.

There were plenty of valuable things scattered about the house, but they were bulky—hard for a thief to remove.   Although Frances did not know just what her father's treasure consisted of, she believed it must be of such a nature that it could be removed by a thief.

Frances, her eyes now well used to the gloom, hurried along in the wake of the drifting shadow, without sound. She came to the first window opening into her father's sleeping apartment. Like a wraith she glided in, believing at last that her duty was to awaken her father.

But when she reached his bed she found it undisturbed. It seemed his pillow had not been lain upon that night. She felt swiftly over the smooth bed, and with growing alarm—not for herself, but alarm for the missing man.

Where could he have gone? What had happened here since the lights went out and that mysterious marauder had come in over the ranch-house roof?

CHAPTER VI

A DIFFERENCE OF OPINION

FRANCES knew her way about her father's room in the dark as well as she did about her own. She knew where every piece of furniture stood. She knew where the chair was on which he carelessly threw his outer clothing at night.

Like most men who for years have slept in the open, Captain Rugley did not remove all his clothing when he went to bed. He usually lay between blankets on the outside of his bed, with his boots and trousers ready to jump into at a moment's notice. Of some of the practices of his life on the plains, with the dome of heaven for a roof-tree, he could not be broken.

She fumbled for the chair, and found it empty. She reached for the belt and holster which he usually hung on a hook at the head of the bed. They, too, were gone, and Frances felt relieved.

She did not withdraw from the room through either of the long windows. Instead, she crept through her father's office and out of the door of that room into the great, main hall.

49

Along this a little way was the door of the room
to which Pratt Sanderson had been assigned, and
that of the treasure room as well.

Frances scarcely gave Pratt a thought. She
presumed him far in the land of dreams. She did
not take into consideration the fact that about
now the scratches of the mountain lion would become painful, and Pratt correspondingly restless.
Frances was mainly troubled by her father's
absence from his room. Had he, too, seen the
mysterious shadow in the court? Was he on the
watch for a possible marauder?

By feeling rather than eyesight she knew the
door to the treasure room was closed. Was her
father there?

She doubled her fist and raised it to knock upon
the panel. Then she hesitated. The slightest
sound would ring through the silent house like an
alarm of fire.

Inclining her ear to the door, she listened. But
the oak planking was thick and there was no
crevice, now the portal was closed, through which
any slight sound could penetrate. She could not
have even distinguished the heavy breathing of a
sleeping man behind the door.

Uncertain, wondering, yet quite mistress of herself again, Frances went on along the corridor.
Here was an open door before her into the court.

Had that shadow she had seen come this way? she wondered.

The hiss of a voice, almost in her ear, *did* startle her:

" My goodness! is it you, Miss Frances? "

A clammy hand clutched her wrist. She knew that Pratt Sanderson must have been horribly wrought up and nervous, for he was trembling.

" What is the matter? Why are you out of your bed, Pratt? " she asked, quite calmly.

" I couldn't sleep. Fever in those scratches, I s'pose," said the young man. " I got up and went outside to get a drink at the fountain—and to bathe my face and wrists. Isn't it hot? "

" You *are* feverish," whispered Frances, cautiously. " Have you seen daddy? "

" The Captain? " returned Pratt, wonderingly. "Oh, no. He isn't up, is he? "

" He's not in his room—— "

" And you're not in yours," said Pratt, with a nervous laugh. " We all seem to be out of our beds at the hour when graveyards yawn, eh? "

Frances had a reassuring laugh ready.

" I think you would better go to bed again, Pratt," she said. " You—you saw nothing in the court? "

" No. But I thought I heard a big bird overhead when I was splashing the water about out

there.   Imagination, of course," he added.
" There are no big night-flying birds out here on
the plains? "

" Not that I know of," returned she.

" I made some noise.   I didn't know what it
was I scared up.   Seemed to be on the roof of the
house."

Frances thought of the mysterious man and his
rope ladder.   But she did not mention them to
Pratt.

" Put some more of father's salve on those
scratches," she advised.   " It's an Indian salve
and very healing.   He was taught by an old
Indian medicine man to make it."

" All right.   Good-night, Miss Frances," said
Pratt, and withdrew into his room, from which he
had appeared so suddenly to accost her.

Pratt's mention of " the bird on the roof " disturbed Frances a good deal.   She turned to run
back upstairs and learn if the ladder was still hanging from the eaves.   But as she started to do so
she realized that the door of the treasure room
had been silently opened.

" Frances ! "

" Oh, Dad ! "

" What are you running about the house for
at this time o' night? " he demanded.

She laughed rather hysterically.   " Why are

you out of your bed, sir—with your rheumatism?"
she retorted.

"Good reason. Thought I heard something,"
growled the Captain.

"Good reason. Thought I *saw* something,"
mocked Frances, seizing his arm.

She stepped inside the room with him. He
flashed an electric torch for a moment about the
place. She saw he had a cot arranged at one
side, and had evidently gone to bed here, beside
the treasure chest.

"Why is this, sir?" she demanded, with pretty
seriousness.

"Reckon the old man's getting nervous," said
Captain Rugley. "Can't sleep in my reg'lar bed
when there are strangers in the house."

Frances started. "What do you mean?" she
cried.

"Well, there's that young man."

"Why, Pratt is all right," declared Frances,
confidently.

"I don't know anything *for* him—and do know
one thing *against* him," growled the old ranchman. "He's been up and about all night, so far.
Weren't you just talking to him?"

"Oh, yes, Dad! But Pratt is all right."

"That's as may be. What was he doing wandering around that court?"

"Oh, Dad! Don't worry about *him*. His arm and chest hurt him—— "

" Humph! didn't hurt him when he went to bed, did they? Yet he was sneaking along this hall and looking into this very room when the door was slightly ajar. I saw him," said the old ranchman, bitterly.

Frances was amazed by this statement; but she realized that her father was oversuspicious regarding the interest of strangers in the old Spanish chest and its contents.

" Never mind Pratt," she said. " I came downstairs to find you, Daddy, because there really *is* a stranger about the house."

" What do you mean, Frances? " was the sharp retort.

The girl told him briefly about the man she had observed climbing up to the veranda roof, and later to the roof of the house by aid of the rope ladder.

" And Pratt tells me he heard some sound up there. He thought it was a big bird," she concluded.

" Come on! " said her father, hastily. " Let's see that ladder."

He locked the door of the treasure room and strode up the main stairway. Frances kept close behind him and warned him to step softly—rather

an unnecessary bit of advice to an old Indian
trailer like Captain Rugley!

But when they came to the window through
which Frances had seen the dangling ladder it was
gone. The old ranchman shot a ray of his electric
torch through the opening; but the light revealed
nothing.

" Gone ! " he announced, briefly.

" Do—do you think so, Dad ? "

" Sure.   Been scared off."

" But what could he possibly want—climbing
up over our roof, and all that ? "

Captain Rugley stood still and stroked his chin
reflectively.   " I reckon I know what they're
after—— "

" They?   But, Daddy, there was only one
man."

" One that was coming over the roof," said her
father.   " But he had pals—sure he did!   If one
of them wasn't in the house—— "

" Why, Dad ! " exclaimed Frances, in wonder.

" You can't always tell," said the old ranchman, slowly.   " There's a heap of valuables in
that chest.   Of course, they don't all belong to
me," he added, hastily.   " My partner, Lon, has
equal rights in 'em—don't ever forget that,
Frances, if something should happen to me."

" Why, Dad ! how you talk ! " she exclaimed.

"We can never tell," sighed her father. "Treasure is tempting. And it looks to me as though this fellow who climbed over the roof expected to find somebody inside to help him. That's the way it looks to me," he repeated, shaking his head obstinately.

"Dear Dad! you don't mean that you think Pratt Sanderson would do such a thing?" said Frances, in a horrified tone.

"We don't know him."

"But his coming here to the Bar-T was unexpected. I urged him to come. That lion really scratched him——"

"Yes. It doesn't look reasonable, I allow," admitted her father; but she could see he was not convinced of the honesty of Pratt Sanderson.

There was a difference of opinion between Frances and Captain Rugley.

CHAPTER VII

THE STAMPEDE

THE remainder of the night passed in quietness. That there really had been a marauder about the Bar-T ranch-house could not be doubted; for a slate was found upon the ground in the morning, and the place in the roof where it had been broken out was plainly visible.

Captain Rugley sent one of the men up with a ladder and new slates to repair the damage. He reported that the marks of the grappling-hook in the roof sheathing were unmistakable, too.

Although her father had expressed himself as doubtful of the good intentions of Pratt Sanderson, Frances was glad to see at breakfast that he treated the young man no differently than before. Pratt slept late and the meal was held back for him.

" The attentions of that old mountain lion bothered me so that I did not sleep much the fore part of the night," Pratt explained.

" How about that bird you heard on the roof? " the Captain asked, calmly.

"I don't know what it was.   It sounded like big wings flapping," the young fellow explained. "But I really didn't see anything."

Captain Rugley grunted, and said no more.   He grunted a good deal this morning, in fact, for every movement gave him pain.

"The rheumatism has got its fangs set in me right, this time," he told Frances.

"That's for being out of your warm bed and chasing all over the house without a coat on in the night," she said, admonishingly.

"Goodness!" said her father.   "Must I be *that* particular?   If so, I *am* getting old, I reckon."

She made him promise to keep out of draughts when she mounted Molly to ride away on an errand to a distant part of the ranch.   She rode off with Pratt Sanderson, for he was traveling in the same direction, toward Mr. Bill Edwards' place.

Frances of the ranges was more silent than she had been when they rode together the night before. Pratt found it hard to get into conversation with her on any but the most ephemeral subjects.

For instance, when he hinted about Captain Rugley's adventures on the Border:

"Your father is a very interesting talker.   He has seen and done so much."

" Yes," said Frances.

" And how adventurous his life must have been! I'd love to get him in a story-telling mood some day."

" He doesn't talk much about old times."

" But, of course, you know all about his adventures as a Ranger, and his trips into Mexico? "

" No," said Frances.

" Why! he spoke last night as though he often talked about it. About the looting of—— Who was the old Spanish grandee he mentioned? "

" I know very little about it, Pratt," fluttered Frances. " That's just dad's talk."

" But that gorgeous girdle and bracelet you wore! "

Frances secretly determined not to wear jewelry from the treasure chest again. She had never thought before about its causing comment and conjecture in the minds of people who did not know her father as well as she did.

Suppose people believed that Captain Dan Rugley had actually stolen those things in some raid into Mexico? Such a thought had never troubled her before. But she could see, now, that strangers might misjudge her father. He talked so recklessly about his old life on the Border that he might easily cause those who did not know him to believe that not alone the contents of that mysterious treasure chest but his other wealth was gained by questionable means.

Fortunately, a herd of steers, crossing from one of the extreme southern ranges of the Bar-T to the north where jucier grass grew, attracted the attention of the guest from Amarillo.

" Are those all yours, Frances? " he asked, when he saw the mass of dark bodies and tossing horns that appeared through rifts in the dust cloud that accompanies a driven herd even over sodland.

" My father's," she corrected, smiling. " And only a small herd.   Not more than two thousand head in that bunch."

" I'd call two thousand cows a whole lot," Pratt sighed.

" Not for us.   Remember, the Bar-T has been in the past one of the great cattle ranches of the West.   Daddy is getting old now and cannot attend to so much work."

" But you seem to know all about it," said Pratt, with enthusiasm.   " Don't you really do all the overseeing for him? "

" Oh, no! " laughed Frances.   " Not at all. Silent Sam is the ranch manager.   I just do what either dad or Sam tell me.   I'm just errand girl for the whole ranch."

But Pratt knew better than that.   He saw now

that she was watching the oncoming mass of steers
with a frown of annoyance. Something was going
wrong and Frances was troubled.

" What's.the matter? " he asked, curiously.

" I thought that was Ratty M'Gill with that
bunch," Frances answered, more as though thinking aloud than consciously answering Pratt's question. " The rascal! He'd run all the fat off a
bunch of cows between pastures."

She pulled Molly around and headed the pinto
for the herd. It was not in his way, but Pratt
followed her example and rode his grey hard after
the cowgirl.

Not a herdsman was in sight. The steers were
coming on through the dust, sweating and steam-
ing, evidently having been driven very hard since
daybreak. Occasionally one bawled an angry pro-
test; but those in front were being forced on by
the rear ranks, which in turn were being harassed
by the punchers in charge.

Suddenly, a bald-faced steer shot out of the ruck
of the herd, darting at right angles to the course.
For a little way a steer can run as fast as a race-
horse. That's why the creatures are so very hard
to manage on occasion.

To Pratt, who was watching sharply, it was a
question which got into action first—Frances or
her wise little pinto. He did not see the girl

speak to Molly; but the pony turned like a shot and whirled away after the careering steer. At the same moment, it seemed, Frances had her hair rope in her hand.

The coils began to whirl around her head. The pinto was running like the wind. The bald-faced, ugly-looking brute of a steer was soon running neck and neck with the well-mounted girl.

Pratt followed. He was more interested in the outcome of the chase than he was in where his grey was putting his feet.

There was an eerie yell behind them. Pratt saw a wild-looking, hatless cowboy racing a black pony toward them. The whole herd seemed to have been turned in some miraculous way, and was thundering after Old Baldface and the girl.

Pratt began to wonder if there was not danger. He had heard of a stampede, and it looked to him as though the bunch of steers was quite out of hand. Had he been alone, he would have pulled out and let the herd go by.

But either Frances did not see them coming, or she did not care. She was after that bald-faced steer, and in a moment she had him.

The whirling noose dropped and in some wonderful way settled over a horn and one of the steer's forefeet. When Molly stopped and braced herself, the steer pitched forward, turned a complete somersault, and lay on the prairie at the mercy of his captor.

"Hurray!" yelled Pratt, swinging his hat.

He was riding recklessly himself. He had seen a half-tamed steer roped and tied at an Amarillo street fair; but *that* was nothing like this. It had all been so easy, so matter-of-fact! No display at all about the girl's work; but just as though she could do it again, and yet again, as often as the emergency arose.

Frances cast a glowing smile over her shoulder at him, as she lay back in the saddle and let Molly hold Old Baldface in durance. But suddenly her face changed—a flash of amazed comprehension chased the triumphant smile away. She opened her lips to shout something to Pratt—some warning. And at that instant the grey put his foot into a ground-dog hole, and the young man from Amarillo left the saddle!

He described a perfect parabola and landed on his head and shoulders on the ground. The grey scrambled up and shot away at a tangent, out of the course of the herd of thundering steers. He was not really hurt.

But his rider lay still for a moment on the prairie. Pratt Sanderson was certainly "playing in hard luck" during his vacation on the ranges.

The mere losing of his mount was not so bad;

but the steers had really stampeded, and he lay, half-stunned, directly in the path of the herd.

Old Baldface struggled to rise and seized upon the girl's attention. She used the rope in a most expert fashion, catching his other foreleg in a loop, and then catching one of his hind legs, too. He was secured as safely as a fly in a spider-web.

Frances was out of her saddle the next moment, and ran back to where Pratt lay. She knew Molly would remain fixed in the place she was left, and sagging back on the rope.

The girl seized the young man under his armpits and started to drag him toward the fallen steer. The bulk of Old Baldface would prove a protection for them. The herd would break and swerve to either side of the big steer.

But one thing went wrong in Frances' calculations. Her rope slipped at the saddle. For some reason it was not fastened securely.

The straining Molly went over backward, kicking and squealing as the rope gave way, and the big steer began to struggle to his feet.

CHAPTER VIII

IN PERIL AND OUT

PRATT SANDERSON had begun to realize the situation. As Frances' pony fell and squealed, he scrambled to his knees.

" Save yourself, Frances! " he cried. " I am all right."

She left him; but not because she believed his statement. The girl saw the bald-faced steer staggering to its feet, and she knew their salvation depended upon the holding of the bad-tempered brute.

The stampeded herd was fast coming down upon them; afoot, she nor Pratt could scarcely escape the hoofs and horns of the cattle.

She saw Ratty M'Gill on the black pony flying ahead of the steers; but what could one man do to turn two thousand head of wild cattle? Frances of the ranges had appreciated the peril which threatened to the full and at first glance.

The prostrate carcase of the huge steer would serve to break the wave of cattle due to pass over this spot within a very few moments. If Baldface got up, shook off the entangling rope and ran, Frances and Pratt would be utterly helpless.

Once under the hoofs of the herd, they would be pounded into the prairie like powder, before the tail of the stampede had passed.

Frances, seeing the attempts of the big steer to climb to its feet, ran forward and seized the rope that had slipped through the ring of her saddle. She drew in the slack at once; but her strength was not sufficient to drag the steer back to earth.

Snorting and bellowing, the huge beast was all but on his feet when Pratt Sanderson reached the girl's side.

Pratt was staggering, for the shock of his fall had been severe. He understood her, however, when she cried:

" Jump on it, Pratt!   Jump on it! "

The young man leaped, landing with both feet on the taut rope.   Frances, at the same instant, threw herself backward, digging her heels into the sod.

The shock of the tightening of the rope, there-- fore, fell upon the steer.   Down he went bellow- ing angrily, for he had not cast off the noose that entangled him.

" Don't let him get loose, Pratt!   Stand on the rope! " commanded Frances.

With the slack of the lariat she ran forward,

caught a kicking hind foot, then entangled one of
the beast's forefeet, and drew both together with
all her strength.   The bellowing steer was now
doubly entangled; but he was not secure, and well
did Frances know it.

She ran in closer, although Pratt cried out in
warning, and looped the rope over the brute's
other horn.   Slipping the end of her rope through
the loop that held his feet together, Frances got a
purchase by which she could pull the great head
of the beast aside and downward, thus holding
him helpless.   It was impossible for him to get
up after he was thus secured.

"Got him!   Quick, Pratt, this way!" Frances
panted.

She beckoned to the Amarillo young man, and
the latter instantly joined her.   She had conquered
the steer in a few seconds; the herd was now thundering down upon them.   M'Gill, on the black
pony, dashed by.

"Bully for you, Miss Frances," he yelled.

"You wait, Ratty!" Frances said; but, of
course, only Pratt heard.   "Father and Sam will
jack you up for this, and no mistake!"

Then she whipped out her revolver and fired it
into the air—emptying all the chambers as the
herd came on.

The steers broke and passed on either side of

their fallen brother.   The tossing horns, fiery eyes
and red, expanded nostrils made them look—to
Pratt's mind—fully as savage as had the mountain lion the evening before.

Then he looked again at his comrade. She was
only breathing quickly now; she gave no sign of
fear.   It was all in the day's work.   Such adventures as this had been occasional occurrences with
Frances of the ranges since childhood.

Pratt could scarcely connect this alert, vigorous
young girl with her who had sat at the piano in the
ranch-house the previous evening!

"You're a wonder!" murmured Pratt Sanderson, to himself.   And then suddenly he broke out
laughing.

"What's tickling you, Pratt?" asked Frances,
in her most matter-of-fact tone.

"I was just wondering," the Amarillo young
man replied, "what Sue Latrop will think of you
when she comes out here."

"Who's she?" asked Frances, a little puzzled
frown marring her smooth forehead. She was
trying to remember any girl of that name with
whom she had gone to school at the Amarillo
High.

"Sue Latrop's a distant cousin of Mrs. Bill
Edwards, and she's from Boston. She's Eastern
to the tips of her fingers—and talk about 'cul-

chaw'! She has it to burn," chuckled Pratt.
"Bill Edwards says she is just 'putting on dog'
to show us natives how awfully crude we are. But
I guess she doesn't know any better."

The steers had swept by, and Pratt was just a
little hysterical. He laughed too easily and his
hand shook as he wiped the perspiration and dust
from his face.

"I shouldn't think she would be a nice girl at
all," Frances said, bluntly.

"Oh, she's not at all bad. Rather pretty and
—my word—some dresser! No end of clothes
she's brought with her. She's coming out to the
Edwards ranch before long, and you'll probably
see her."

Frances bit her lip and said nothing for a
moment. The big steer struggled again and
groaned. The girl and Pratt were afoot and the
stampede of cattle had swept their mounts away.
Even Molly, the pinto, was out of call.

The half dozen punchers who followed the
maddened steers had no time for Frances and
her companion. A great cloud of dust hung over
the departing herd and that was the last the cast-
aways on the prairie would see of either cattle or
punchers that day.

"We've got to walk, I reckon," Frances said,
slowly.

"How about this steer?" asked the young man, curiously.

"I think he's tamed enough for the time," said the girl, with a smile. "Anyway I want my rope. It's a good one."

She began to untangle the bald-faced steer. He struggled and grunted and tossed his wide, wicked horns free. To tell the truth Pratt was more than a little afraid of him. But he saw that Frances had reloaded the revolver she carried, and he merely stepped aside and waited. The girl knew so much better what to do that he could be of no assistance.

"Now, Pratt," she said, at last, "stand from under! Hoop-la!"

She swung the looped lariat and brought it down smartly upon the beast's back as it struggled to its shaking legs. The steer bellowed, shook himself like a dog coming out of the water, or a mule out of the harness, and trotted away briskly.

"He'll follow the herd, I reckon," Frances said, smiling again. "If he doesn't they'll pick him out at the next round-up. His brand is too plain to miss."

"And now we're afoot," said Pratt. "It's a long walk for you back to the house, Frances."

"And longer for you to the Edwards ranch," she laughed. "But perhaps you will fall in with some of Mr. Bill's herders. They'll have an extra mount or two. I'll maybe catch Molly. She's a good pinto."

" But oughtn't I to go back with you? " questioned Pratt, doubtfully. "You see—you're alone—and afoot—— "

" Why! it isn't the first time, Pratt," laughed the girl. " Don't fret about me. This range to me is just like your backyard to you."

" I suppose it sounds silly," admitted Pratt. " But I haven't been used to seeing girls quite as independent as you are, Frances Rugley."

" No? The girls you know don't live the sort of life I do," said the range girl, rather wistfully.

" I don't know that they have anything on you," put in Pratt, stoutly. "I think you're just wonderful! "

" Because I am doing something different from what you are used to seeing girls do," she said, with gravity. " That is no compliment, Pratt."

" Well! I meant it as such," he said, earnestly. He offered his hand, knowing better than to urge his company upon her. " And I hope you know how much obliged to you I am. I feel as though you had saved my life twice. I would not have known what to do in the face of that stampede."

" Every man to his trade," quoted Frances, carelessly. " Good-bye, Pratt. Come over again to see us," and she gave his hand a quick clasp and turned away briskly.

He stood and watched her for some moments; then, fearing she might look back and see him, he faced around himself and set forth on his long tramp to the Edwards ranch.

It was true Frances did not turn around; but she knew well enough Pratt gazed after her. He would have been amazed had he known her reason for showing no further interest in him—for not even turning to wave her hand at him in good-bye. There were tears on her cheeks, and she was afraid he would see them.

"I am foolish—wicked!" she told herself. "Of course he knows other—and nicer—girls than *me*. And it isn't just that, either," she added, rather enigmatically. "But to remember all those girls I knew in Amarillo! How different their lives are from mine!

"How different they must look and behave. Why, I'm a perfect *tomboy*. Pratt said I was wonderful—just as though I were a trick pony, or an educated goose!

"I do things he never saw a girl do before, and he thinks it strange and odd. But if that Sue Latrop should see me and say that I was not nice, he'd begin to see, too, that it is a fact.

"Riding with the boys here on the ranch, and

officiating at the branding-pen, riding herd, cutting
out beeves and playing the cowboy generally, has
not added to my ' culchaw,' that is sure. I don't
know that I'd be able to ' act up ' in decent society
again.

" Pratt looked at me big-eyed last evening
when I dressed for dinner. But he was only
astonished and amused, I suppose. He didn't
expect me to look like that after seeing me in this
old riding dress.

" Oh, dear ! " sighed Frances of the ranges. " I
wouldn't leave daddy, or do anything to displease
him, poor dear ! But I wish he could be content
to live nearer to civilization.

" We've got enough money. *I* don't want any
more, I'm sure. We could sell the cattle and turn
our ranges into wheat and milo fields. Then we
could live in town part of the year—in Amarillo,
perhaps ! "

The thought was a daring one. Indeed, she
was not wholly confident that it was not a wicked
thought.

Just then she reached the summit of a slight
ridge from which she could behold the home corrals
of the *hacienda* itself, still a long distance ahead,
and glowing like jewels in the morning sunshine.

Such a beautiful place ! After all, Frances
Rugley loved it. It was home, and every tender

tie of her life bound her to it and to the old man who she knew was sitting somewhere on the veranda, with his pipe and his memories.

There never was such another beautiful place as the old Bar-T! Frances was sure of that. She longed for Amarillo and what the old Captain called "the frills of society"; but could she give up the ranch for them?

"I reckon I want to keep my cake and eat it, too," she sighed. "And that, daddy would say, 'is plumb impossible!'"

FRANCES WHIPPED OUT HER REVOLVER AND FIRED IT INTO
THE AIR.   ·   ·   *Page 67.*

CHAPTER IX

FRANCES arrived at home about noon. The last few miles she bestrode Molly, for that intelligent creature had allowed herself to be caught. It was too late to go on the errand to Cottonwood Bottom before luncheon.

Silent Sam Harding met her at the corral gate. He was a lanky, saturnine man, with never a laugh in his whole make-up. But he was liked by the men, and Frances knew him to be faithful to the Bar-T interests.

"What happened to Ratty's bunch?" he asked, in his sober way.

"Did you see them?" cried Frances, leaping down from the saddle.

"Saw their dust," said Sam.

"They stampeded," Frances said, warmly. "And Mr. Sanderson and I lost our ponies—pretty nearly had a bad accident, Sam," and she went on to give the foreman of the ranch the particulars.

75

"I thought something was wrong. I got that little grey hawse of Bill Edwards'. He just come in," said Sam.

"Ratty M'Gill was running those steers," Frances told him. "I must report him to daddy. He's been warned before. I think Ratty's got some whiskey."

"I shouldn't wonder. There was a bootlegger through here yesterday."

"The man who tried to get over our roof!" exclaimed Frances.

"Mebbe."

"Do you suppose he's known to Ratty?" questioned the girl, anxiously.

"Dunno. But Ratty's about worn out his welcome on the Bar-T. If the Cap says the word, I'll can him."

"Well," said Frances, "he shouldn't have driven that herd so hard. I'll have to speak to daddy about it, Sam, though I hate to bother him just now. He's all worked up over that business of last night."

"Don't understand it," said the foreman, shaking his head.

"Could it have been the bootlegger?" queried Frances, referring to the illicit whiskey seller of whom she suspected the irresponsible Ratty M'Gill had purchased liquor. The "bootleggers" were supposed to carry pint flasks of bad whiskey in the legs of their topboots, to sell at a fancy price to thirsty punchers on the ranges.

" Dunno how that slate come broken on the roof," grumbled Sam. " The feller knowed just where to go to hitch his rope ladder. Goin' to have one of the boys ride herd on the *hacienda* at night for a while." This was a long speech for Silent Sam.

Frances thanked him and went up to the house. She did not find an opportunity of speaking to Captain Rugley about Ratty M'Gill at once, however, for she found him in a state of great excitement.

" Listen to this, Frances! " he ejaculated, when she appeared, waving a sheet of paper in his hand, and trying to get up from the hard chair in which he was sitting.

A spasm of pain balked him; his bronzed face wrinkled as the rheumatic twinge gripped him; but his hawklike eyes gleamed.

" My! my! " he grunted. " This pain is something fierce."

Frances fluttered to his side. "Do take an easier chair, Daddy," she begged. " It will be so much more comfortable."

" Hold on! this does very well. Your old dad's never been used to cushions and do-funnies.

But see here! I want you to read this." He waved the paper again.

"What is it, Daddy?" Frances asked, without much curiosity.

"Heard from old Lon at last—yes, ma'am! What do you know about that? From good old Lon, who was my partner for twenty years. I've got a letter here that one of the boys brought from the station just now, from a minister, back in Mississippi. Poor old Lon's in a soldier's home, and he's just got track of me.

"My soul and body, Frances! Think of it," added the excited Captain. "He's been living almost like a beggar for years in a Confederate soldiers' home—good place, like enough, of its kind, but here am I rolling in wealth, and that treasure chest right here under my eye, and Lon suffering, perhaps——"

The Captain almost broke down, for with the pain he was enduring and all, the incident quite unstrung him. Frances had her arms about him and kissed his tear-streaked cheek.

"Foolish, am I?" he demanded, looking up at her. "But it's broken me up—hearing from my old partner this way. Read the letter, Frances, won't you?"

She did so. It was from the chaplain of the Bylittle Soldiers' Home, of Bylittle, Mississippi.

" CAPTAIN DANIEL RUGLEY,
  " Bar-T Ranch,
    " Texas Panhandle.
" DEAR SIR:

  " I am writing in behalf of an old soldier in this institution, one Jonas P. Lonergan, who was at one time a member of Company K, Texas Rangers, and who before that time served honorably in Company P, Fifth Regiment, Mississippi Volunteers, during the War between the States.

  " Mr. Lonergan is a sadly broken man, having passed through much evil after his experiences on the Border and in Mexico in your company. Indeed, his whole life has been one of privation and hardship. Now, bent with years, he has been obliged to seek refuge with some of his ancient comrades at Bylittle.

  " In several private talks with me, Captain Rugley, he has mentioned the incidents relating to the looting and destruction of Señor Morales' *hacienda,* over the Border in Mexico, while you and he were on detail in that vicinity as Rangers.

  " Perhaps the old man is rambling; but he always talks of a treasure chest which he claims you and he rescued from the bandits and removed into Arizona, hiding the same in a certain valley at the mouth of a cañon which he calls Dry Bone Cañon.

" Mr. Lonergan always speaks of you as ' the whitest man who ever lived.' ' If my old partner, Captain Dan, knew how I was fixed or where I was, he'd have me rollin' in luxury in no time,' he has said to me; ' providing he's this same Captain Dan Rugley that's owner of the Bar-T Ranch in the Panhandle.'

" You know (if you know him at all) that Mr. Lonergan had no educational advantages.   Such men have difficulty in keeping up communication with their friends.

" He claims to have lost track of you twenty-odd years ago.   That when you separated you both swore to divide equally the contents of Señor Morales' treasure chest, the hiding place of which at that time was in a hostile country, Geronimo and his braves being on the warpath.

" If you are Jonas P. Lonergan's old-time part-ner you will remember the particulars more clearly than I can state them.

" If this be the case, I am sure I need only state the above and certify to the identity of Mr. Loner-gan, to bring from you an expression of your remembrance and the statement whether or no any property to which Mr. Lonergan might make a claim is in your possession.

" Mr. L. speaks much of the treasure chest and tells marvelous stories of its contents.   He does not seem to desire wealth for himself, however, for he well knows that he has but a few months to live, nor does he seem ever to have cared greatly for money.

" His anxiety is for the condition of a sister of his who was left a widow some years ago, and for her son. Mr. L. fears that the nephew has not the chance of getting on in life that he would like the boy to have. In his old age Mr. L. feels keenly the fact that he was never able to do anything for his family, and the fate of his widowed sister and her son is much on his mind.

" A prompt reply, Captain Rugley, if you are the old-time partner of my ancient friend, will be gratefully received by the undersigned, and joyfully by Mr. Lonergan.

" Respectfully,
" (Rev.) DECIMUS TOOLEY."

" Why! what do you think of that? " gasped Frances, when she had read the letter to the very last word.

Her father's face was shining and there were tears in his eyes. His joy at hearing from his old companion-in-arms was unmistakable.

This turning up of Jonas Lonergan meant the parting with a portion of the mysterious wealth that the old ranchman kept hidden in the Spanish chest—wealth that he might easily keep if he would.

Frances was proud of him. Never for an instant did he seem to worry about parting with the treasure to Lonergan. His fears for it had never been the fears of a miser who worshiped wealth—no, indeed!

Now it was plain that the thought of seeing his old partner alive again, and putting into his hands the part of the treasure rightfully belonging to him, delighted Captain Dan Rugley in every fibre of his being.

"The poor old codger!" exclaimed the ranchman, affectionately. "And to think of Lon being in need, and living poor—maybe actually suffering —when I've been doing so well here, and have had this old chest right under my thumb all these years.

"You see, Frances," said the Captain, making more of an explanation than ever before, "Lon and I got possession of that chest in a funny way.

"We'd been sent after as mean a man as ever infested the Border—and there were some mighty mean men along the Rio Grande in those days. He had slipped across the Border to escape us; but in those times we didn't pay much attention to the line between the States and Mexico.

"We went after him just the same. He was with a crowd of regular bandits, we found out.

And they were aiming to clean up Señor Milo Morales' *hacienda*.

" We got onto their plans, and we rode hard to the *hacienda* to head them off. We knew the old Spaniard—as fine a Castilian gentleman as ever stepped in shoe-leather.

"We stopped with him a while, beat off the bandits, and captured our man. After everything quieted down (as we thought) we started for the Border with the prisoner. Señor Morales was an old man, without chick or child, and not a relative in the world to leave his wealth to. His was one of the few Castilian families that had run out. Neither in Mexico nor in Spain did he have a blood tie.

" His vast estates he had already willed to the Church. Such faithful servants as he had (and they were few, for the *peon* is not noted for gratitude) he had already taken care of.

"Lon and I had saved his life as well as his personal property, he was good enough to say, and he showed us this treasure chest and what was in it. When he passed on, he said, it should be ours if we were fixed so we could get it before the Mexican authorities stepped in and grabbed it all, or before bandits cleaned out the *hacienda*. It was a toss-up in those days between the two, which was the most voracious!

" Well, Frances, that's how it stood when we rode away with Simon Hawkins lashed to a pony between us. Before we reached the river we heard of a big band of outlaws that had come down from the Sierras and were trailing over toward Morales'.

" We hurried back, leaving Simon staked down in a hide-out we knew of. But Lon and I were too late," said the old Captain, shaking his head sadly. " Those scoundrels had got there ahead of us, led by the men we had first beaten off, and they had done their worst.

" The good old Señor—as harmless and lovely a soul as ever lived—had been brutally murdered. One or two of his servants had been killed, too— for appearance's sake, I suppose. The others, especially the *vaqueros,* had joined the outlaws, and the *hacienda* was being looted.

" But Lon and I took a chance, stole in by night, found the treasure chest, and slipped away with it. I went back alone before dawn, found a six-mule team already loaded with household stuff and drove off with it, thus stealing from the thieves.

" A good many of these fine old things we have here were on that wagon. I decided that they belonged to me as much as to anybody. Get them once over the boundary into God's country and the thieving Mexican Government—only one degree

removed at that time from the outlaws themselves
—would not dare lay claim to them.

"We did this," concluded Captain Dan, with a
sigh of reminiscence, and with his eyes shining,
"and we got Simon into the jail at Elberad, too.

"Lon and I kept on up into Arizona, into Dry
Bone Cañon, and there we cached the stuff.   Air
and sand are so dry there that nothing ever decays,
and so all these rugs and hangings and feather work
were uninjured when I brought them away to this
ranch soon after you were born.

"That's the story, my dear.   I never talk much
about it, for it isn't altogether my secret.   You
see, my old partner, Lon, was in on it.   And now
he's going to come for his share——"

"Come for his share, Daddy?" asked Frances,
in surprise.

"Yes—sir-ree—sir!" chuckled the old ranchman.   "Think I'm going to let old Lon stay in
that soldiers' home?   Not much!"

"But will he be able to travel here to the Panhandle?"

"Of course!   What the matter is with Lon,
he's been shut indoors.   I know what it is.   Why!
he's younger than I am by a year or two."

"But if he can't travel alone——"

"I'll go after him!   I'll hire a private car!
My goodness!   I'll hire a whole train if it's neces-

sary to get him out of that Bylittle place! That's what I'll do!

" And he shall live here with us—so he shall! He and I will divide this treasure just as I've been aching to do for years. You shall have jewels then, my girl! "

" But, dear! " gasped Frances, "you are not well enough to go so far."

" Now, don't bother, Frances. Your old dad isn't dead yet—not by any means! I'll be all right in a day or two."

But Captain Rugley was not all right in so short a time. He actually grew worse. Frances sent a messenger for the doctor the very next morning. Whether it was from the exposure of the night the stranger tried to climb over the *hacienda* roof or not, Captain Rugley took to his bed. The physician pronounced it rheumatic fever, and a very serious case indeed.

CHAPTER X

THE MAN FROM BYLITTLE

RESPONSIBILITY weighed heavily upon the young shoulders of Frances of the ranges in these circumstances.

Old Captain Rugley insisted upon being out of doors, ill as he was, and they made him as comfortable as possible on a couch in the court where the fountain played. Ming was in attendance upon him all day long, for Frances had many duties to call her away from the ranch-house at this time. But at night she slept almost within touch of the sick man's bed.

He did not get better. The physician declared that he was not in immediate danger, although the fever would have to run its course. The pain that racked his body was hard to bear; and although he was a stoic in such matters, Frances would see his jaws clench and the muscles knot in his cheeks; and she often wiped the drops of agony from his forehead while striving to hide the tears that came into her own eyes.

He demanded to know how long he was " going

to be laid by the heels "; and when he learned that the doctor could not promise him a swift return to health, Captain Rugley began to worry.

It was of his old partner he thought most. That the affairs of the ranch would go on all right in the hands of his young daughter and Silent Sam, he seemed to have no doubt. But the letter from the chaplain of the Bylittle Soldiers' Home was forever troubling him. Between his spells of agony, or when his mind was really clear, he talked to Frances of little but Jonas Lonergan and the treasure chest.

" He is troubling his mind about something, and it is not good for him," the doctor, who came every third day (and had a two hundred-mile jaunt by train and buckboard), told Frances. " Can't you calm his mind, Miss Frances? "

She told the medical man as much about her father's ancient friend as she thought was wise. " He desires to have him brought here," she explained, " so that they can go over, face to face and eye to eye, their old battles and adventures."

" Good! Bring the man—have him brought," said the physician.

" But he is an old soldier," said Frances. She read aloud that part of the Reverend Decimus Tooley's letter relating to the state of Mr. Lonergan's health.

" Don't know what we can do about it, then,"
said the doctor, who was a native of the Southwest
himself.   " Your father and the old fellow seem
to be 'honing' for each other.   Too bad they
can't meet.   It would do your father good.   I
don't like his mind's being troubled."

That night Frances was really frightened.   Her
father began muttering in his sleep.   Then he
talked aloud, and sat up in bed excitedly, his face
flushed, and his tongue becoming clearer, although
his speech was not lucid.

He was going over in his distraught mind the
adventures he had had with Lon when they two had
foiled the bandits and recovered possession of the
Señor's treasure chest.

Frances begged him to desist, but he did not
know her.   He babbled of the long journey with
the mule team into the mouth of Dry Bone Cañon,
and the caching of the treasure.   For an hour he
talked steadily and then, growing weaker, gradually sank back on his pillows and became silent.

But the effort was very weakening.   Frances
telephoned from the nearest station for the doctor.
Something *had* to be done, for the exertion and
excitement of the night had left Captain Rugley in
a state that troubled the girl much.

She had no friend of her own sex.   Mrs. Bill
Edwards was a city woman whom, after all, she

scarcely knew, for the lady had not been married to Mr. Edwards more than a year.

There were other good women scattered over the ranges—some "nesters," some small cattle-raisers' wives, and some of the new order of Pan-handle farmers; but Frances had never been in close touch with them.

The social gatherings at the church and school-house at Jackleg had been attended by Frances and Captain Rugley; but the Bar-T folk really had no near neighbors.

The girl's interest in the forthcoming pageant had called the attention of other people to her more than ever before; but to tell the truth the young folk were rather awe-stricken by Frances' abilities as displayed in the preparation for the entertainment, while the older people did not know just how to treat the wealthy ranchman's daughter—whether as a person of mature years, or as a child.

Riding back from the railroad station, where one of the boys with the buckboard three hours later would meet the physician, she thought of these facts. Somehow, she had never felt so lonely—so cut off from other people as she did right now.

The railroad crossed one corner of the Bar-T's vast fenced ranges; but there were twenty long miles between the house and the station. She had ridden Molly hard coming over to speak to the doctor on the telephone; but she took it easy going back.

Somewhere along the trail she would meet the buckboard and ponies going over to meet the doctor. And as she walked her pony down the slope of the trail into Cottonwood Bottom, she thought she heard the rattle of the buckboard wheels ahead.

A clump of trees hid the trail for a bit; when she rounded it the way was empty. Whoever she had heard had turned off the trail into the cotton-woods.

" Maybe he didn't water the ponies before he started," thought Frances, " and has gone down to the ford. That's a bit of carelessness that I do not like. Whom could Sam have sent with the bronchos for the doctor? "

She turned Molly off the trail beyond the bridge. The wood was not a jungle, but she could not see far ahead, nor be seen. By and by she smelled tobacco smoke—the everlasting cigarette of the cattle puncher. Then she heard the sound of voices.

Why this latter fact should have made Frances suspicious, she could not have told. It was her womanly intuition, perhaps.

Slipping out of the saddle, she tied Molly with her head up-wind. She was afraid the pinto would smell her fellows from the ranch, and signal them, as horses will.

Once away from her mount, she passed between the trees and around the brush clumps until she saw the ford of the river sparkling below her. There were the hard-driven ponies, their heads drooping, their flanks heaving, standing knee-deep in the stream—this fact in itself an offense that she could not overlook.

The animals had been overdriven, and now the employee of the ranch who had them in charge was allowing them to cool off too quickly—and in the cold stream, too!

But who was he? For a moment Frances could not conceive.

The figure of the driver was humped over on the seat in a slouching attitude, sitting sideways, and with his back toward the direction from which the range girl was approaching. He faced a man on a shabby horse, whose mount likewise stood in the stream and who had been fording the river from the opposite direction.

This horseman was a stranger to Frances. He wore a broad-brimmed black hat, no chaps, no cartridge belt or gun in sight, and white shirt and a vest under his coat, while shoes instead of boots were on his feet. He was neither puncher nor farmer in appearance. And his face was bad.

There could be no doubt of that latter fact. He wore a stubble of beard that did not disguise the sneering mouth, or the wickedly leering expression of his eyes.

"Well, I done my part, old fellow," drawled the man in the seat of the buckboard, just as Frances came within earshot. "'Tain't my fault you bungled it."

Frances stopped instead of going on. It was Ratty M'Gill!

She could not understand why he was not on the range, or why Sam had sent the ne'er-do-well to meet the doctor. It puzzled her before the puncher's continued speech began to arouse her curiosity.

"You'll sure find yourself in a skillet of hot water, old fellow," pursued Ratty, inhaling his cigarette smoke and letting it forth through his nostrils in little puffs as he talked. "The old Cap's built his house like a fort, anyway. And he's some man with a gun—believe me!"

"You say he's sick," said the other man, and he, too, drawled. Frances found herself wondering where she had heard that voice before.

"He ain't so sick that he can't guard that chest you was talkin' about. He's had his bed made up right in the room with it. That's whatever," said Ratty.

"Once let me get in there," said the other, slowly.

"Sam's set some of the boys to ride herd on the house," chuckled Ratty.

"That's the way, then!" exclaimed the other, raising his clenched fist and shaking it. "You get put on that detail, Ratty."

"I'll see you blessed first," declared the puncher, laughing. "I don't see nothing in it but trouble for me."

"No trouble for you at all. They didn't get you before."

"No," said the puncher. "More by good luck than good management. I don't like going things blind, Pete. And you're always so blamed secretive."

"I have to be," growled the other. "You're as leaky as a sieve yourself, Ratty. I never could trust you."

"Nor nobody else," laughed the reckless puncher. "Sam's about got my number now. If he ain't the gal has——"

"You mean that daughter of the old man's?"

"Yep. She's an able-minded gal—believe me! And she's just about boss of the ranch, specially now the old Cap is laid by the heels for a while."

The other was silent for some moments.   Ratty gathered up the reins from the backs of the tired ponies.

" I gotter step along, Pete," he said.   " Gal's gone to telephone for the medical sharp, who'll show up on Number 20 when she goes through Jackleg.   I'm to meet him.   Or," and he began to chuckle again," José Reposa was, and I took his place so's to meet you here as I promised."

" And lots of good your meeting me seems to do me," growled the man called Pete.

" Well, old fellow! is that my fault? " demanded the puncher.

" I don't know.   I gotter git inside that *hacienda.*"

" Walk in.   The door's open."

" You think you are smart, don't you? " snarled Pete, in anger.   " You tell me where the chest is located; but it couldn't be brought out by day.   But at night——   My soul, man! I had the team all ready and waiting the other night, and I could have got the thing if I'd had luck."

" You didn't have luck," chuckled Ratty M'Gill. " And I don't believe you'd 'a' had much more luck if you'd got away with the old Cap's chest."

" I tell you there's a fortune in it! "

" You don't know—— "

" And I suppose you do? " snarled Pete.

"I know no sane man ain't going to keep a whole mess of jewels and such, what you talk about, right in his house. He'd take 'em to a bank at Amarillo, or somewhere."

"Not that old codger. He'd keep 'em under his own eye. He wouldn't trust a bank like he would himself. Humph! I know his kind.

"Why," continued Pete, excitedly, "that old feller at Bylittle is another one just like him. These old-timers dug gold, and made their piles half a dozen times, and never trusted banks—there warn't no banks!"

"Not in them days," admitted Ratty. "But there's a plenty now."

"You say yourself he's got the chest."·

"Sure! I seen it once or twice. Old Spanish carving and all that. But I bet there ain't much in it, Pete."

"You'd ought to have heard that doddering old idiot, Lonergan, talk about it," sniffed Pete. "Then your mouth would have watered. I tell you that's about all he's been talkin' about the last few months, there at Bylittle. And I was orderly on his side of the barracks and heard it all.

"I know that the parson, Mr. Tooley, was goin' to write to this Cap Rugley. Has, before now, it's likely. Then something will be done about the treasure—— "

"Waugh!" shouted Ratty. "Treasure! You sound like a silly boy with a dime story book."

The puncher evidently did not believe his friend knew what he was talking about. Pete glowered at him, too angry to speak for a minute or two.

Frances began to worm her way back through the brush. She put the biggest trees between her and the ford of the river. When she knew the two men could not see or hear her, she ran.

She had heard enough. Her mind was in a turmoil just then. Her first thought was to get away, and get Molly away. Then she would think this startling affair out.

CHAPTER XI

SHE got away from the Bottom without disturbing Ratty and the man from Bylittle. Once Molly
was loping over the plain again, Frances began to
question her impressions of the dialogue she had
overheard.

In the first place, she was sure she had heard
the voice of the man, Pete, before. It was the
same drawling voice that had come out of the
darkness asking for food and a bed the evening
Pratt Sanderson stopped at the Bar-T Ranch.

The voice had been cheerful then; it was snarling now; but the tones were identical. Then,
going a step farther, Frances realized, from the
talk she had just heard, that this Pete was the man
who had tried to get over the roof of the ranch-
house. One and the same man—tramp and robber.

Ratty had shown Pete the way. Ratty was a
traitor. He might easily have seen the broken
slate on the roof and pointed it out to the mysterious Pete.

The latter had been an orderly in the Bylittle Soldiers' Home, and had heard the story of the Spanish treasure chest, when old Mr. Lonergan was rambling about it to the chaplain.

The fellow's greed had started him upon the quest of the treasure so long in Captain Rugley's care. Perhaps he had known Ratty M'Gill before; it seemed so. And yet, Ratty did not seem entirely in the confidence of the robber.

Nevertheless, Ratty must leave the ranch. Frances was determined upon this.

She could not tell her father about him; and she shrank from revealing the puncher's villainy to Silent Sam Harding. Indeed, she was afraid of what Sam and the other boys on the ranch might do to punish Ratty M'Gill. The Bar-T punchers might be rather rough with a fellow like Ratty.

Frances believed the boys on the Bar-T were loyal to her father and herself. Ratty's defection hurt her as much as it surprised her. She had never thought him more than reckless; but it seemed he had developed more despicable characteristics.

These and similar thoughts disturbed Frances' mind as she made her way back to the ranch-house. She found her father very weak, but once more quite lucid. Ming glided away at her approach, and Frances sat down to hold the old ranchman's hand and tell him inconsequential things regarding the work on the ranges, and the gossip of the bunk-house.

All the time the girl's heart hungered to nurse him herself, day and night, instead of depending upon the aid of a shuffle-footed Chinaman. The mothering instinct was just as strong in her nature as in most girls of her age. But she knew her duty lay elsewhere.

Before this time Captain Rugley had never entirely given over the reins of government into the hands of Silent Sam. He had kept in touch with ranch affairs, delegating some duties to Frances, others to Sam or to the underforeman. Now the girl had to be much more than the inter-mediary between the old ranchman and his em-ployees.

The doctor had impressed her with the rule that his patient was not to be worried by business mat-ters. Many things she had to do " off her own bat," as Sam Harding expressed it. The matter of Ratty M'Gill's discharge must be one of these things, Frances saw plainly.

She waited now for the doctor's appearance with much anxiety of mind. The Captain was quiet when the physician came; but the effect of his delirium of the night before was plain to the medical eye.

" Something must be done to ease his mind of
this anxiety about his old chum, Frances," said the
doctor, taking her aside. " That, I take it, was
the burden of his trouble when he rambled last
night in his speech? "

" Yes, sir."

" Try to get the fellow brought here, then,"
said the doctor, with decision.

" That Mr. Lonergan? "

" The old soldier—yes. Can't it be done? "

" I—I don't know," said the troubled girl.
" The chaplain writes that he is a sick man—— "

" And so is your father. I warn you. A very
sick man. And he cannot be moved, while this
Lonergan can probably travel if his fare is paid."

" Oh, Doctor! If it is only a matter of money,
father, I know, would hire a private car—a whole
train, he said!—to get his old partner here,"
Frances declared.

" Good! I advise you to go ahead and send
for the man," said the physician. " It's the best
prescription for Captain Rugley that I can give
you. He has his mind set upon seeing his old
friend, and these delirious spells will be repeated
unless his longing is satisfied. And such attacks
are weakening."

" Oh, I see that, Doctor! " agreed Frances.

She sat down that very hour and wrote to the

Reverend Decimus Tooley, explaining why she, instead of Captain Rugley, wrote, and requesting that Jonas Lonergan be made ready for the trip from Bylittle to Jackleg, in the Panhandle, where a carriage from the Bar-T Ranch would meet him.

She told the chaplain of the soldiers' home that a private car would be supplied for Captain Rugley's old partner to travel in, if it were necessary. She would make all arrangements for transportation immediately upon receiving word from Mr. Tooley that the old man could travel.

Haste was important, as she explained. Likewise she asked the following question—giving no reason for her curiosity:

" Did there recently leave the Bylittle Home an employee—an orderly—whose first name is Peter? And if so, what is his reputation, his full name, and why did he leave the Home? "

" Maybe that will puzzle the Reverend Mr. Tooley some," thought Frances of the ranges. " But I am indeed curious about this friend of Ratty M'Gill's. And now I'll tell Silent Sam that there is a man lurking about the Bar-T who must be watched."

She said nothing to Captain Rugley about sending for Lonergan until she had written. The doctor said it would be just as well not to discuss the matter much until it was accomplished. He also left soothing medicine to be given to the patient if he again became delirious.

Frances was so much occupied with her father all that day that she could do nothing about Ratty M'Gill. She had noticed, however, that the Mexican boy, José Reposa, had driven the doctor to the ranch and that he took him back to the train again.

The reckless cowpuncher had somehow bribed the Mexican boy to let him take his place on the buckboard that forenoon.

"Ratty is like a rotten apple in the middle of the barrel," thought Frances. "If I let him remain on the ranch he will contaminate the other boys. No, he's got to go!

"But if I tell him why he is discharged it will warn him—and that Pete—that we suspect, or know, an attempt is being made to rob father's old chest. Now, what shall I do about this?"

The conversation between Ratty and Pete at the ford which she had overheard gave Frances an idea. She saw that the contents of the treasure chest ought really to be put into a safety deposit vault in Amarillo. But the old ranchman considered it his bounden duty to keep the treasure in his own hands until his partner came to divide it; and he would be stubborn about any change in this plan.

Lonergan could not get to the Bar-T for three weeks, or more. In the meantime suppose Pete made another attempt to steal the contents of the Spanish chest?

Frances Rugley felt that she could depend upon nobody in this emergency for advice; and upon few for assistance in carrying out any plan she might make to thwart those bent upon robbing the *hacienda*. To see the sheriff would advertise the matter to the public at large. And that, she well knew, would make Captain Dan Rugley very angry.

Whatever she did in this matter, as well as in the affair of Ratty M'Gill, must be done without advice.

Her mind slanted toward Pratt Sanderson at this time. Had her father not seemed to suspect the young fellow from Amarillo, Frances would surely have taken Pratt into her confidence.

Now that Captain Rugley had given a clear explanation of how he had come possessed of a part of the loot of Señor Milo Morales' *hacienda*, Frances was not afraid to take a friend into her confidence.

There was no friend, however, that she cared to confide in save Pratt. And it would anger her father if she spoke to the young fellow about the treasure.

She knew this to be a fact, for when Pratt Sanderson had ridden over from the Edwards Ranch
to inquire after Captain Rugley's health, the old
ranchman had sent out a courteously worded
refusal to see Pratt.

" I'm not so awfully fond of that young chap,"
the Captain said, reflectively, at the time.   " And
seems to me, Frances, he's mighty curious about
my health."

" But, Daddy! " Frances cried, " he was only
asking out of good feeling."

" I don't know that," growled the old ranchman.   " I haven't forgotten that he was here in
the house the night that other fellow tried to
break in.   Looks curious to me, Frances—sure
does! "

She might have told him right then about Ratty
M'Gill and the man Pete; but Frances was not an
impulsive girl.   She studied about things, as the
colloquialism has it.   And she knew very well that
the mere fact that Ratty and the stranger were
friends would not disprove Pratt's connection with
the midnight marauder.   Pete might have had an
aid inside, as well as outside, the *hacienda.*

So Frances said nothing more to the old ranchman, and nothing at all to Pratt about that which
troubled her.   They spoke of inconsequential
things on the veranda, where Ming served cool

drinks; and then the Amarillo young man rode away.

" Sue Latrop and that crowd will be out to-morrow, I expect," he said, as he departed. " Don't know when I can get over again, Frances. I'll have to beau them around a bit."

" Good-bye, Pratt," said Frances, without comment.

" By the way," called Pratt, from his saddle and holding in his pony, " your father being so ill isn't going to make you give up your part in the pageant, Frances? "

" Plenty of time for that," she returned, but without smiling. " I hope father will be well before the date set for the show."

Pratt's departure left Frances with a sinking heart; but she did not betray her feelings. To be all alone with her father and the two Chinamen at the ranch-house seemed hard indeed; and with the responsibility of the treasure chest on her heart, too!

Her father, it was true, had insisted on having his couch placed at night in the room with the Spanish chest. He seemed to consider that, ill as he was, he could guard the treasure better than anybody else.

Frances had to devise a plan without either her father's advice or that of anybody else. She prepared for the adventure by begging the Captain to have burlap wrapped about the chest and securely roped on.

" Then it won't be so noticeable," she told him, " when people come in to call on you." For some of the other cattlemen of the Panhandle rode many miles to call at the Bar-T Ranch; and, of course, they insisted upon seeing Captain Rugley.

Ming and San Soo (the latter was very tall and enormously strong for a coolie) corded the Spanish chest as directed, and under the Captain's eye. Then Frances threw a Navajo blanket over it and it looked like a couch or divan.

To Silent Sam she said; " I want a four-mule wagon to go to Amarillo for supplies. When can I have it?"

" Can't you have the goods come by rail to Jackleg?" asked the foreman, somewhat surprised by the request.

Now, Jackleg was not on the same railroad as Amarillo. Frances shook her head.

" I'm sorry, Sam. There's something particular I must get at Amarillo."

" You going with the wagon, Miss Frances?"

" Yes. I want a good man to drive —Bender, or Mack Hinkman. None of the Mexicans will do. We'll stop at Peckham's Ranch and at the hotel in Calas on the way."

" Whatever ye say," said Sam. " When do ye want to go? "

" Day after to-morrow," responded Frances, briskly. " It will be all right then? "

" Sure," agreed Silent Sam. " I'll fix ye up."

Frances had several important things to do before the time stated. And, too, before that time, something quite unexpected happened.

CHAPTER XII

MOLLY

FRANCES' secret plans did not interfere with her usual tasks. She started in the morning to make her rounds. Molly had been resting and would now be in fine fettle, and the girl expected to call her to the gate when she came down to the corral in which the spare riding stock was usually kept.

Instead of seeing only José Reposa or one of the other Mexicans hanging about, here was a row of punchers roosting along the top rail of the corral fence, and evidently so much interested in what was going on in the enclosure that they did not notice the approach of Captain Rugley's daughter.

" Better keep off 'n the leetle hawse, Ratty! " one fellow was advising the unseen individual who was partly, at least, furnishing the entertainment for the loiterers.

" She looks meek," put in another, " but believe me! when she was broke, it was the best day's work Joe Magowan ever done on this here ranch. Ain't that so, boys? "

" Ratty warn't here then," said the first speaker.

"He don't know that leetle Molly hawse and what capers she done cut up—— "

" Molly!" ejaculated Frances, under her breath, and ran forward.

At that instant there was a sudden hullabaloo in the corral. Some of the men cheered; others laughed; and one fell off the fence.

" Go it!"

" Hold tight, boy!"

" Tie a knot in your laigs underneath her, Ratty! She's a-gwine to try to throw ye clean ter Texarkana!"

" *What's he doing with my pony?* "

The cry startled the string of punchers. They turned—most of them looking sheepish enough—and gaped, wordlessly, at Frances, who came running to the fence.

Molly was her pet, her own especial property. Nobody else had ridden the pinto since she was broken by the head wrangler, Joe Magowan. Nor was Molly really broken, in the ordinary acceptation of the term.

Frances could ride her—could do almost anything with her. She was the best cutting-out pony on the ranch. She was gentle with Frances, but she had never shown fondness for anybody else, and would look wall-eyed on the near approach of anybody but the girl herself. None but Joe and

Frances had ever bridled her or cinched the saddle
on Molly.

Ratty M'Gill was the culprit, of course; nor did
he hear Frances' cry as she arrived at the corral.
He had bestridden the nervous pinto and Molly
was " acting up."

Ratty had his rope around her neck and a loop
around her lower jaw, as Indians guide their half-
wild steeds. At every bound the puncher jerked
the pony's jaw downward and raked her flanks
with his cruel spurs. These latter were leaving
welts and gashes along the pinto's heaving sides.

" You cruel fellow ! " shrieked Frances. " Get
off my pony at once ! "

" Say ! she's trying to buck, Miss Frances," one
of the men warned her. " She'll be sp'il't if he
lets her beat him now. You won't never be able
to ride her, once let her git the upper hand."

" Mind you own concerns, Jim Bender ! " exclaimed the girl, both wrathful and hurt. " I can
manage that pony if she's let alone." Then she
raised her voice again and cried to Ratty:

" M'Gill ! you get off that horse ! At once, I tell
you ! "

" The Missus is sure some peeved," muttered
Bender to one of his mates.

" And why shouldn't she be? We'd never
ought to let Ratty try to ride that critter."

"Molly!" shouted Frances, climbing the fence herself as quickly as any boy.

She dropped over into the corral where the other ponies were running about in great excitement.

"Molly, come here!" She whistled for the pinto and Molly's head came up and her eyes rolled in the direction of her mistress. She knew she was being abused; and she remembered that Frances was always kind to her.

Whether Ratty agreed or not, the pinto galloped across the corral.

"Get down off that pony, you brute!" exclaimed Frances, her eyes flashing at the half-serious, half-grinning cowboy.

"She's some little pinto when she gits in a tantrum," remarked the unabashed Ratty.

Frances had brought her bridle. Although Molly stood shaking and quivering, the girl slipped the bit between her jaws and buckled the straps in a moment. She held the pony, but did not attempt to lead her toward the saddling shed.

"M'Gill," Frances said, sharply, "you go to Silent Sam and get your time and come to the house this noon for your pay. You'll never bestride another pony on this ranch. Do you hear me?"

"What's that?" demanded the cowpuncher, his

face flaming instantly, and his black eyes sparkling.

She had reproved him before his mates, and the young man was angry on the instant. But Frances was angry first. And, moreover, she had good reason for distrusting Ratty. The incident was one lent by Fortune as an excuse for his discharge.

" You are not fit to handle stock," said Frances, bitingly. " Look what you did to that bunch of cattle the other day! And I've watched you more than once misusing your mount. Get your pay, and get off the Bar-T. We've no use for the like of you."

" Say! " drawled the puncher, with an ugly leer. " Who's bossing things here now, I'd like to know? "

" I am! " exclaimed the girl, advancing a step and clutching the quirt, which swung from her wrist, with an intensity that turned her knuckles white. " You see Sam as I told you, and be at the house for your pay when I come back."

The other punchers had slipped away, going about their work or to the bunk-house. Ratty M'Gill stood with flaming face and glittering eyes, watching the girl depart, leading the trembling Molly toward the exit of the corral.

" You're a sure short-tempered gal this A. M.,"

he growled to himself. " And ye sure have got it in for me.   I wonder why?   I wonder why?"

Frances did not vouchsafe him another look. She stood in the shadow of the shed and petted Molly, fed her a couple of lumps of sugar from her pocket, and finally made her forget Ratty's abuse.   But Molly's flanks would be tender for some time and her temper had not improved by the treatment she had received.

" Perfectly scandalous!" exclaimed Frances, to herself, almost crying now.   " Just to show off before the other boys.   Oh! he was mean to you, Molly dear!   A fellow like Ratty M'Gill will stand watching, sure enough."

Finally, she got the saddle cinched upon the nervous pinto and rode her out of the corral and away to the ranges for her usual round of the various camps.   She had not been as far as the West Run for several days.

CHAPTER XIII

THE GIRL FROM BOSTON

COW-PONIES are never trained to trot. They walk if they are tired; sometimes they gallop; but usually they set off on a long, swinging lope from the word "Go!" and keep it up until the riders pull them down.

The moment Frances of the ranges had swung herself into Molly's saddle, the badly treated pinto leaped forward and dashed away from the corrals and bunk-house. Frances let her have her head, for when Molly was a bit tired she would forget the sting and smart of Ratty M'Gill's spurs and quirt.

Frances had not seen Silent Sam that morning; but was not surprised to observe the curling smoke of a fresh fire down by the branding pen. She knew that a bunch of calves and yearlings had been rounded up a few days before, and the foreman of the Bar-T would take no chance of having them escape to the general herds on the ranges, and so have the trouble of cutting them out again at the grand round-up.

It was impossible, even on such a large ranch as the Bar-T, to keep cattle of other brands from running with the Bar-T herds. A breach made in a fence in one night by some active young bull would allow a Bar-T herd and some of Bill Edwards' cattle, for instance, to become associated.

To try to separate the cattle every time such a thing happened would give the punchers more than they could do. The cattle thus associated were allowed to run together until the round-up. Then the unbranded calves would always follow their mothers, and the herdsmen could easily separate the young stock, as well as that already branded, from those belonging on other ranches.

Although it was a bit out of her direct course, Frances pulled Molly's head in the direction of the branding fire. Before she came in sight of the bawling herd and the bunch of excited punchers, a cavalcade of riders crossed the trail, riding in the same direction.

No cowpunchers these, but a party of horsemen and horsewomen who might have just ridden out of the Central Park bridle-path at Fifty-ninth Street or out of the Fens in Boston's Back Bay section.

At a distance they disclosed to Frances' vision—unused to such sights—a most remarkable jumble of colors and fashions. In the West khaki, brown, or olive grey is much worn for riding togs by the women, while the men, if not in overalls, or chaps, clothe themselves in plain colors.

But here was actually more than one red coat! A red coat with never a fox nearer than half a thousand miles!

" Is it a circus parade? " thought Frances, setting spurs to her pinto.

And no wonder she asked. There were three girls, or young women, riding abreast, each in a natty red coat with tails to it, hard hats on their heads, and skirts. They rode side-saddle. Luckily the horses they rode were city bred.

There were two or three other girls who were dressed more like Frances herself, and bestrode their ponies in sensible style. The males of the party were in the Western mode; Frances recognized one of them instantly; it was Pratt Sanderson.

He was not a bad rider. She saw that he accompanied one of the girls who wore a red coat, riding close upon her far side. The cavalcade was ambling along toward the branding pen, which was in the bottom of a coulie.

As Frances rode up behind the party, Molly's little feet making so little sound that her presence was unnoticed, the Western girl heard a rather shrill voice ask:

"And what are they doing it for, Pratt? I re'lly don't just understand, you know. Why burn the mark upon the hides of those—er—embryo cows?"

"I'm telling you," Pratt's voice replied, and Frances saw that it was the girl next to him who had asked the question. " I'm telling you that all the calves and young stock have to be branded."

"Branded?"

"Yes. They belong to the Bar-T, you see; therefore, the Bar-T mark has to be burned on them."

"Just fancy!" exclaimed the girl in the red coat. "Who would think that these rude cattle people would have so much sentiment. This Frances Rugley you tell about owns all these cows? And does she have her monogram burned on all of them?"

Frances drew in her mount. She wanted to laugh (she heard some of the party chuckling among themselves), and then she wondered if Pratt Sanderson was not, after all, making as much fun of her as he was of the girl in the red coat?

Pratt suddenly turned and saw the ranchman's daughter riding behind them. He flushed, but smiled, too; and his eyes were dancing.

"Oh, Sue!" he exclaimed. "Here is Frances now."

So this was Sue Latrop—the girl from Boston. Frances looked at her keenly as she turned to look at the Western girl.

" My dear! Fancy! So glad to know you," she said, handling her horse remarkably well with one hand and putting out her right to Frances.

The latter urged Molly nearer. But the pinto was not on her good behavior this morning. She had been too badly treated at the corral.

Molly shook her head, danced sideways, wheeled, and finally collided with Pratt's grey pony. The latter squealed and kicked. Instantly, Molly's little heels beat a tattoo on the grey's ribs.

" Hello! " exclaimed Pratt, recovering his seat and pulling in the grey. " What's the matter with that horse, Frances? "

Molly was off like a rocket. Frances fairly stood in the stirrups to pull the pinto down—and she was not sparing of the quirt. It angered her that Molly should " show off " just now. She had heard Sue Latrop's shrill laugh.

When she rode back Frances did not offer to shake hands with the Boston girl. And, as it chanced, she never did shake hands with her.

" You ride such perfectly ungovernable horses out here," drawled the Boston girl. " Is it just for show? "

"Our ponies are not usually family pets," laughed Frances. Yet she flushed, and from that moment she was always expecting Sue to say cutting things.

"They tell me it is so interesting to see the calves—er—monogrammed; do you call it?" said Sue, with a little cough.

"Branded!" exclaimed Pratt, hurriedly.

"Oh, yes! So interesting, I suppose?"

"We do not consider it a show," said Frances, bluntly. "It is a necessary evil. I never fancied the smell of scorched hair and hide myself; and the poor creatures bawl so. But branding and slitting their ears are the only ways we have of marking the cattle."

"Re'lly?" repeated Sue, staring at her as though Frances were more curious than the bawling cattle.

The irons were already in the fire when the party rode down to the scene of the branding. Silent Sam was in charge of the gang. They had rounded up nearly two hundred calves and yearlings. Some of the cows had followed their offspring out of the herd, and were lowing at the corral fence.

Afoot and on horseback the men drove the half-wild calves into the branding pen runway. As they came through they were roped and thrown, and

Sam and an assistant clapped the irons to their bony hips. The smell of singed hair was rather unpleasant, and the bawling of the excited cattle drowned all conversation.

When a calf or a yearling was let loose, he ran as hard as he could for a while, with the smoking " monogram," as Sue Latrop called it, the object of his tenderest attention. But the smart of it did not last for long, and the branded stock soon went to graze contentedly outside the corral fence, forgetting the experience.

Frances had a chance to speak to Sam for a moment.

" Ratty will come to you for his time. I'm going to pay him off this noon. I've got good reason for letting him go."

" I bet ye," agreed Sam, for whatever Frances said or did was right with him.

Pratt insisted upon Frances meeting all these people from Amarillo. There was Mrs. Bill Edwards, whom she already knew, as chaperon. Most of the others were young people, although nearer Pratt's age than that of the ranchman's daughter.

Sue Latrop was the only one from the East. She had been to Amarillo before, and she evidently had much influence over her girl friends from that Panhandle city, if over nobody else. Two of the girls had copied her riding habit exactly; and if imitation is the sincerest flattery, then Sue was flattered indeed.

The Boston girl undoubtedly rode well. She had had schooling in the art of sticking to a side-saddle like a fly on a wall!

Her horse curvetted, arched his neck, played pretty tricks at command, and was long-legged enough to carry her swiftly over the ground if she so desired. He made the scrubby, nervous little cow-ponies—including Molly—look very shabby indeed.

Sue Latrop apparently believed she was ever so much better mounted than the other girls, for she was the only one who had brought her own horse. The others, including Pratt, were mounted on Bill Edwards' ponies.

While they were standing in a group and talking, there came a yell from the branding pen. A section of rail fence went down with a crash. Through the fence came a little black steer that had escaped several " branding soirées."

Blackwater, as the Bar-T boys called him, was a notorious rebel. He was originally a maverick —a stray from some passing herd—and had joined the Bar-T cattle unasked. That was more than two years before. He had remained on the Bar-T ranges, but was evidently determined in his dogged

mind not to submit to the humiliation of the brand-
ing-iron.

He had been rounded up with a bunch of yearlings and calves a dozen times; but on each occasion had escaped before they got him into the
corral. It was better to let the black rebel go than
to lose a dozen or more of the others while chasing him.

This time, however, Silent Sam had insisted
upon riding the rebel down and hauling him, bawling, into the corral.

But the rope broke, and before the searing-iron
could touch the black steer's rump he went
through the fence like a battering-ram.

"Look out for that ornery critter, Miss
Frances!" yelled the foreman of the Bar-T
Ranch.

Frances saw him coming, headed for the group
of visitors. She touched Molly with the spur, and
the intelligent cow-pony jumped aside into the
clear-way. Frances seized the rope hanging at her
saddle.

Pratt had shouted a warning, too. The visitors
scattered. But for once Sue Latrop did not manage her mount to the best advantage.

"Look out, Sue!"

"Quick! He'll have you!"

These and other warnings were shouted. With

lowered front the black steer was charging the horse the girl from Boston rode.

Unlike the trained cow-ponies from Bill Edwards' corral, this gangling creature did not know, of himself, what to do in the emergency. The other mounts had taken their riders immediately out of the way. Sue's horse tossed his head, snorted, and pawed the earth, remaining with his flank to the charging steer.

" Get out o' that! " yelled Pratt, and laid his quirt across the stubborn horse's quarters.

But to no avail. Sue could neither manage him nor get out of the saddle to escape Blackwater. The maverick was fortunately charging the strange horse from the off side, and he was coming like a shot from a cannon.

The cowpunchers at the pen were mounting their ponies and racing after the black steer, but they were too far away to stop him. In another moment he would head into the body of Sue's mount with an awful impact!

CHAPTER XIV.

THE CONTRAST

" FRANCES ! "

Pratt Sanderson fairly shrieked the ranch girl's name. He could do nothing to save Sue Latrop himself, nor could the other visitors from Amarillo. Silent Sam and his men were too far away.

If with anybody, it lay with Frances Rugley to save the Boston girl. Frances already had her rope circling her head and Molly was coming on the jump!

The wicked little black steer was almost upon the gangling Eastern horse ere Frances stretched forward and let the loop go.

Then she pulled back on Molly's bridle reins. The cow-pony began to slide, haunches down and forelegs stiffened. The loop dropped over the head of the black steer.

Had Blackwater been a heavier animal, he would have overborne Frances and her mount at the moment the rope became taut. For it was not a good job at all—that particular roping Frances was afterward ashamed of.

To catch a big steer in full flight around the neck only is to court almost certain disaster; but Blackwater did not weigh more than nine hundred pounds.

Nor was Molly directly behind him when Frances threw the lariat. The rope tautened from the side—and at the very instant the mad steer collided with Sue Latrop's mount.

The wicked head of the steer banged against the horse's body, which gave forth a hollow sound; the horse himself squealed, stumbled, and went over with a crash.

Fortunately Sue had known enough to loosen her foot from the stirrup. As Frances lay back in her own saddle, and she and Molly held the black steer on his knees, Pratt drove his mount past the stumbling horse, and seized the Boston girl as she fell.

She cleared her rolling mount with Pratt's help. Otherwise she would have fallen under the heavy carcase of the horse and been seriously hurt.

Blackwater had crashed to the ground so hard that he could not immediately recover his footing. He kicked with a hind foot, and Frances caught the foot expertly in a loop, and so got the better of him right then and there. She held the brute helpless until Sam and his assistants reached the spot.

It was Pratt who had really done the spectacular thing. It looked as though Sue Latrop owed her salvation to the young man.

"Hurrah for Pratt!" yelled one of the other young fellows from the city, and most of the guests—both male and female—took up the cry. Pratt had tumbled off his own grey pony with Sue in his arms.

"You're re'lly a hero, Pratt! What a fine thing to do," the girl from Boston gasped. "Fancy my being under that poor horse."

The horse in question was struggling to his feet, practically unhurt, but undoubtedly in a chastened spirit. One of the boys from the branding pen caught his bridle.

Pratt objected to the praise being showered upon him. "Why, folks, I didn't do much," he cried. "It was Frances. She stopped the steer!"

"You saved my life, Pratt Sanderson," declared Sue Latrop. "Don't deny it."

"Lots of good I could have done if that black beast had been able to keep right on after your horse, Sue," laughed Pratt. "You ask Mr. Sam Harding—or any of them."

Sue's pretty face was marred by a frown, and she tossed her head. "I don't need to ask them. Didn't you catch me as I fell?"

" Oh, but, Sue—— "

" Of course," said the Boston girl, in a tone quite loud enough for Frances to hear, "those cowmen would back up their employer. They'd say she helped me. But I know whom to thank. You are too modest, Pratt."

Pratt was silenced. He saw that it was useless to try to convince Sue that she was wrong. It was plain that the girl from Boston did not wish to feel beholden to Frances Rugley.

So the young man dropped the subject. He ran after his own pony, and then brought Sue's stubborn mount to her hand. Sue was being congratulated and made much of by her friends. None of them spoke to Frances.

Pratt came over to the latter before she could ride away after the bawling steer. Blackwater was going to be branded this time if it took the whole force of the Bar-T to accomplish it!

" Thank you, Frances, for what you did," the young man said, grasping her hand. " And Bill will thank you, too. He'll know that it was your work that saved her; Mrs. Edwards isn't used to cattle and isn't to be blamed. I feel foolish to have them put it on me."

Frances laughed. She would not show Pratt that this whole series of incidents had hurt her deeply.

" Don't make a mountain out of a mole-hill, Pratt," she said. " And you did do a brave thing. That girl would have been hurt if you had not caught her."

" Oh, I don't know," he grumbled.

" I reckon she thinks so, anyway," said Frances, her eyes twinkling. " How does it feel to be a hero, Pratt? "

Pratt blushed and turned away. " I don't want to wear any laurels that are not honestly my own," he muttered.

" But you don't object to Miss Boston's expression of gratitude, Pratt? " teased Frances.

He made a little face at her as he went back to the ranchman's wife and her guests; without another word Frances spurred Molly in the other direction, and before Mrs. Bill Edwards could speak to her the girl of the ranges was far away.

She headed for the West Run, where a large herd of the Bar-T cattle grazed. Nor did she look back again to see what became of the group of riders who were with Mrs. Edwards and Pratt.

Frances had no heart for such company just then. Sue Latrop's manner had really hurt the Western girl. Perhaps Frances was easily wounded; but Sue had plainly revealed her opinion of the ranchman's daughter.

The contrast between them cut Frances to the

quick. She keenly realized how she, herself, must appear in the company of the pretty Eastern girl.,

"Of course, Pratt, and Mrs. Edwards, and all of them, must see how superior she is to me," Frances thought, as Molly galloped away with her. " But just the same, I don't like that Sue Latrop a bit! "

CHAPTER XV

IN THE FACE OF DANGER

FRANCES was going by the way of Cottonwood Bottom because the trail was better and there were fewer gates to open.

The Bar-T kept a gang riding fence all the time; but even so, it was impossible always to keep up the wires. Frances seldom if ever rode from home without wire cutters and staples in a pocket of her saddle.

She stopped several times on this morning to mend breaks and to tighten slack wires, so it was late when she found the herd at West Run. Here were chuck-wagon, horse corral and camp—a regular " cowboy's home," in fact.

The boss of the outfit was Asa Bird, and Tom Phipps was the wrangler, while a Mexican, named Miguel, was cooking for the outfit.

" Ya-as, Miss Frances," drawled Asa, " I reckon we need a right smart of things. Mike says he's most out o' provisions; but for the love of home don't send us no more beans. We've jest about been beaned to death! No wonder them Greasers are fighting among themselves all the endurin' time. It's the *frijoles* they eat makes 'em so fractious—sure is!"

Frances wrote out a list of the goods needed, for the next supply wagon that passed this way to drop at the camp, and looked over the outfit in general in order to report fully to Sam and her father regarding the conditions at the West Run.

It was high noon before she got in sight of the cottonwoods on her homeward trail. She was hurrying Molly, for she did not want to keep Ratty M'Gill waiting for his money. As she had told him, she wanted the reckless cowboy off the Bar-T ranges before nightfall.

She had struck the plain above the river ford when she sighted a single rider far ahead, and going in her own direction. It was plain that the man—whoever he was—was heading for the ford instead of the bridge where the new trail crossed.

Something about this fact—or about the slouching rider himself—made Frances suspicious. She was reminded of the last time she had come this way and of the dialogue she had overheard between Ratty M'Gill and the man named Pete.

"If he turns to look back, he will see me," thought the excited girl.

Instantly she was off Molly's back. There might be no time to ride out of sight over the ridge. Here was an old buffalo wallow, and she took advantage of it.

In the old days when the bison roamed the plains of the Panhandle the beasts made wallows in which they ground off the grass, and the grass-roots as well, leaving a barren hollow from two to four feet in depth. These dust baths were used frequently by the heavily-coated buffalo in hot weather.

Holding Molly by the head the girl commanded her to lie down. The cow-pony, perfectly amenable to her young mistress now, obeyed the order, grunting as she dropped to her knees, the saddle squeaking.

"Be dead!" ordered Frances, sternly. The pinto rolled on her side, stretched out her neck, and blinked up at the girl. She was entirely hidden from any chance glance thrown back by the stranger on the trail; and when Frances dropped down, too, both of them were well out of sight of any one riding the range.

The range girl waited until she was quite sure the stranger had ridden beyond the first line of cottonwoods. Perhaps he merely wished to water his steed at the ford, but Frances had her doubts of him.

When she finally stood up to scrutinize the plain ahead, there was no moving object in sight. Yet she did not mount and ride Molly when she had got the pinto on its legs.

Instead, she led the pony, and kept off the well-worn trail, too. The pounding of hoofs on a hard trail can be distinguished for a long distance by a man who will take the trouble to put his ear to the ground. The sound travels almost as far as the jar of a coming railroad train on the steel rails.

It was more than two miles to the beginning of the cottonwood grove, and one cannot walk very fast and lead a horse, too. But with a hand on Molly's neck, and speaking an urgent word to the pinto now and then, Frances was able to accomplish the journey within a reasonable time.

Meantime she saw no sign of the man on horseback, nor of anybody else. He had ridden down to the ford, she was sure, and was still down there.

Once among the trees, Frances tied the pinto securely and crept through the thickets toward the shallow part of the stream. She heard no voices this time; but she did smell smoke.

" Not tobacco," thought Frances Rugley, with decision. " He's built a campfire. He is going to stay here for a time. What for, I wonder? Is he expecting to meet somebody? "

This Cottonwood Bottom, as it was called, was on the Bar-T range. Nobody really had business here save the ranch employees. The trail to the

hacienda was not a general road to any other ranch
or settlement. It was curious that this lone man
should come here and make camp.

She came in sight of him ere long. He had
kindled a small fire, over which already was a bat-
tered tin pot in which coffee beans were stewing.
The rank flavor was wafted throught the grove.

His scrubby pony was grazing, hobbled. The
man's flapping hat brim hid his face; but Frances
knew him.

It was Pete, the man who had been orderly at
the Soldiers' Home, at Bylittle, Mississippi, and
who had frankly owned to coming to the Panhandle for the purpose of robbing Captain Dan
Rugley.

The girl of the ranges was much puzzled what
to do in this emergency. Should she creep away, ·
ride Molly hard back to the ranch-house, arouse
Sam and some of the faithful punchers, and with
them capture this ne'er-do-well and run him off
the ranges?

That seemed, on its face, the more sensible if
the less romantic thing to do. Yet the very pub-
licity attending such a move was against it.

The suspicion that Captain Rugley had a treasure hidden away in the old Spanish chest was not
a general one. It might have been lazily discussed
now and then over some outfit's fire when other

subjects of gossip had "petered out," to use the punchers' own expression.

But it was doubtful if even Ratty M'Gill believed the story. Frances had heard him scoff at the man, Pete, for holding such a belief.

If she attempted to capture this tramp by the fire, making the affair one of importance, the story of the Spanish treasure chest would spread over half the Panhandle.

" What the boys didn't know wouldn't hurt them ! " Frances told herself, and she would not ask for help. She had already laid her plans and she would stick to them.

And while she hesitated, discussing these things in her mind, a figure afoot came down the slope toward the ford and the campfire. It was Ratty M'Gill, walking as though already footsore, and with his saddle and accoutrements on his shoulder.

The high-heeled boots worn by cowpunchers are not easy footwear to walk in. And a real cattleman's saddle weighs a good bit ! Ratty flung down the leather with a grunt, and dropped on the ground beside the fire.

" What's the matter with you ? " growled the man, Pete. " Been pulling leather ? "

" There ain't no hawse bawn can make me git off if I don't want," returned Ratty M'Gill, sharply. " I got canned."

" Fired? "

" Yep.   And by that snip of a gal," and he said it viciously.

" Ain't you man enough to have a pony of your own? "

" Sam wouldn't sell me one—the hound!   Nor I didn't have no money to spare for a mount, anyway.   I'd rustle one out of the herd if the wranglers hadn't drove 'em all up the other way las' night.   And I said I'd come over here to see you again."

"What else?" demanded Pete, suspiciously. He seemed to know that Ratty had not come here to the ford for love of him.

" Wal, old man!   I tried to go to headquarters. Went in to see the Cap.   Nothing doing.   If the gal had canned me, that was enough.   So he said, and so Sam Harding said.   I'm through at the Bar-T."

" That's a nice thing," snarled Pete.   " And just as I got up a scheme to use you there! "

" Mebbe you can use me now," grunted Ratty.

" I—don't—know "

" Oh, I seen something that you'd like to know about."

" What is that? " asked Pete, quickly.

The old Cap has taken a tumble to himself. Guess he was put wise by what happened the other

night—you know. He's going to send the chest
to the Amarillo bank."

" *What?* "

" That's so," said Ratty, with his slow drawl,
and evidently enjoying the other's discomfiture.

" How do you know? " snapped Pete.

" Seed it. Standing all corded up and with a
tag on it, right in the hall. Knowed Sam was
going to get ready a four-mule team for Amarillo
to-morrow morning. The gal's going with it, and
Mack Hinkman to drive. Good-night! if there's
treasure in that chest, you'll have to break into
the Merchants' and Drovers' Bank of Amarillo to
get at it—take that from me ! "

Pete leaned toward him and his hairy hand
clutched Ratty's knee. What he said to the discharged employee of the Bar-T Ranch Frances
did not hear. She had, however, heard enough.
She was worried by what Ratty had said about
his interview with Captain Rugley. Her father
should not have been disturbed by ranch business
just then.

The girl crept back through the grove, found
Molly where she had left her, and soon was a
couple of miles away from the ford and making
for the ranch-house at Molly's very best pace.

She found her father not so much excited as she
had feared. Ratty had forced his way into the

stricken cattleman's room and done some talking;
but the Captain was chuckling now over the incident.

"That's the kind of a spirit I like to see you
show, Frances," he declared, patting her hand.
"If those punchers don't do what you tell 'em,
bounce 'em!   They've got to learn what you say
goes—just as though I spoke myself.   And Ratty
M'Gill never was worth the powder to blow him
to Halifax," concluded the ranchman, vigorously.

Frances was glad her father approved of her
action.   But she did not believe they were well rid
of Ratty just because he had started for Jackleg
Station.

She had constantly in mind Ratty and the man,
Pete, with their heads together beside the campfire; and she wondered what villainy they were
plotting.   Nevertheless, in the face of possible
danger, she went ahead with her scheme of start-
ing for Amarillo in the morning.   And, as Ratty
had said, the chest, burlapped, corded, and tagged,
stood in the main hall of the ranch-house, ready
for removal.

CHAPTER XVI

A FRIEND INSISTENT

It was a long way to the Peckham ranch-house, at which Frances meant to make her first night stop. The greater part of the journey would then be over.

The second night she proposed to stay at the hotel in Calas, a suburb of Amarillo. Her errands in the big town would occupy but a few hours, and she expected to be back at Peckham's on the third evening, and at home again by the end of the fourth day.

She was troubled by the thought of being so long away from her father's side; but he was on the mend again and the doctor had promised to see him at least once while she was away from the ranch.

Her reason she gave for going to Amarillo was business connected with the forthcoming pageant, " The Panhandle: Past and Present." This explanation satisfied her father, too—and it was true to a degree.

She heard from the chaplain of the Bylittle Soldiers' Home the day before she was to start on her brief journey, and she sent José Reposa with a long prepaid telegraph message to the station, arranging for a private car in which Jonas P. Lonergan was to travel from Mississippi to the Panhandle. She hoped the chaplain would come with him. About the ex-orderly of the home the letter said nothing. Perhaps Mr. Tooley had overlooked that part of her message.

Captain Rugley was delighted that his old partner was coming West; the announcement seemed to have quieted his mind. But he lay on his bed, watching the corded chest, with his gun hanging close at hand.

That is, he watched one of the corded and burlapped chests. The secret of the second chest was known only to Frances herself and the two Chinamen. Anybody who entered the great hall of the *hacienda* saw that one, as Ratty had, standing ready for removal. The one in Captain Rugley's room was covered by the blanket and looked like an ordinary divan.

Frances believed San Soo and Ming were to be trusted. But to Silent Sam she left the guarding of the ranch-house during her absence.

Day was just beginning to announce itself by faint streaks of pink and salmon color along the eastern horizon, when the four-mule wagon and

Frances' pony arrived at the gate of the compound. The two Chinamen, Sam himself, and Mack Hinkman, the driver, had all they could do to carry the chest out to the wagon.

Frances came out, pulling on her gantlets. She had kissed her father good-bye the evening before, and he was sleeping peacefully at this hour.

"Have a good journey, Miss Frances," said Sam, yawning. "Look out for that off mule, Mack. *Adios.*"

The Chinamen had scuttled back to the house. Frances was mounted on Molly, and the heavy wagon lurched forward, the mules straining in the collars under the admonition of Mack's voice and the snap of his bullwhip.

The wagon had a top, and the flap at the back was laced down. No casual passer-by could see what was in the vehicle.

Frances rode ahead, for Molly was fresh and was anxious to gallop. She allowed the pinto to have her head for the first few miles, as she rode straight away into the path of the sun that rose, red and jovial-looking, above the edge of the plain.

A lone coyote, hungry after a fruitless night of wandering, sat upon its haunches not far from the trail, and yelped at her as she passed. The morning air was as invigorating as new wine, and her cares and troubles seemed to be lightened already.

She rode some distance ahead of the wagon; but
at the line of the Bar-T she picketed Molly and
built a little fire. She carried at her saddle the
means and material for breakfast. When the
slower moving mule team came up with her there
was an appetizing odor of coffee and bacon in the
air.

"That sure does smell good, Ma'am!" declared Mack. "And it's on-expected. I only got
a cold bite yere."

"We'll have that at noon," said Frances,
brightly. "But the morning air is bound to make
one hungry for a hot drink and a rasher of bacon."

In twenty minutes they were on the trail again.
Frances now kept close to the wagon. Once off
the Bar-T ranges she felt less like being out of
sight of Mack, who was one of the most trustworthy men in her father's employ.

He was not much of a talker, it was true, so
Frances had little company but her own thoughts;
but *they* were company enough at present.

As she rode along she thought much about the
pageant that was to be held at Jackleg; many of
the brightest points in that entertainment were
evolved by Frances of the ranges on this long ride
to the Peckham ranch.

There were several breaks in the monotony
of the journey. One was when another covered

wagon came into view, taking the trail far ahead
of them. It came from the direction of Cottonwood Bottom, and was drawn by two very good
horses. It was so far ahead, however, that neither
Frances nor Mack could distinguish the outfit or
recognize the driver.

"Dunno who that kin be," said Mack, "'nless
it's Bob Ellis makin' for Peckham's, too. I
learned he was going to town this week."

Bob Ellis was a small rancher farther south.
Frances was doubtful.

"Would Ellis come by that trail?" she queried.
"And why doesn't he stop to pass the time of
day with us?"

"That's so!" agreed Mack. "It couldn't be
Bob, for he'd know these mules, and he ain't been
to the Bar-T for quite a spell. I dunno who that
kin be, then, Miss Frances."

Frances had had her light fowling-piece put in
the wagon, and before noon she sighted a flock of
the scarce prairie chickens. Away she scampered
on Molly after the wary birds, and succeeded, in
half an hour, in getting a brace of them.

Mack picked and cleaned the chickens on the
wagon-seat. "They'll help out with supper to-
night, if Miz' Peckham ain't expectin' company,"
he remarked.

But they were not destined to arrive at the

Peckham ranch without an incident of more importance than these.

It was past mid-afternoon. They had had their cold bite, rested the mules and Molly, and the latter was plodding along in the shade of the wagon-top all but asleep, and her rider was in a like somnolent condition. Mack was frankly snoring on the wagon-seat, for the mules had naught to do but keep to the trail.

Suddenly Molly lifted her head and pricked her ears. Frances came to herself with a slight shock, too. She listened. The pinto nickered faintly.

Frances immediately distinguished the patter of hoofs. A single pony was coming.

The girl jerked Molly's head around and they dropped back behind the wagon which kept on lumberingly, with Mack still asleep on the seat. From the south—from the direction of the distant river—a rider came galloping up the trail.

"Why!" murmured Frances. "It's Ratty M'Gill!"

The ex-cowboy of the Bar-T swung around upon the trail, as though headed east, and grinned at the ranchman's daughter. His face was very red and his eyes were blurred, and Frances feared he had been drinking.

"Hi, lady!" he drawled. "Are ye mad with me?"

"I don't like you, M'Gill," the girl said, frankly. "You don't expect me to, do you?"

"Aw, why be fussy?" asked the cowboy, gaily. "It's too pretty a world to hold grudges. Let's be friends, Frances."

Frances grew restive under his leering smile and forced gaiety. She searched M'Gill sharply with her look.

"You didn't gallop out of your way to tell me this," she said. "What do you want of me?"

"Oh, just to say how-de-do!" declared the fellow, still with his leering smile. "And to wish you a good journey."

"What do you know about my journey?" asked Frances, quickly.

But Ratty M'Gill was not so much intoxicated that he could be easily coaxed to divulge any secret. He shook his head, still grinning.

"Heard 'em say you were going to Amarillo, before I went to Jackleg," he drawled. "Mighty lonesome journey for a gal to take."

"Mack is with me," said Frances, shortly. "I am not lonely."

"Whew! I bet that hurt me," chuckled Ratty M'Gill. "My room's better than my comp'ny, eh?"

"It certainly is," said the girl, frankly.

"Now, you wouldn't say that if you knowed

something that I know," declared the fellow, grinning slily.

"I don't know that anything you may say would interest me," the girl replied, sharply, and turned Molly's head.

"Aw, hold on!" cried Ratty. "Don't be so abrupt. What I gotter say to you may help a lot."

But Frances did not look back. She pushed Molly for the now distant wagon. In a moment she knew that Ratty was thundering after her. What did he mean by such conduct? To tell the truth, the ranchman's daughter was troubled.

Surely, the reckless fellow did not propose to attack Mack and herself on the open trail and in broad daylight? She opened her lips to shout for the sleeping wagon-driver, when a cloud of dust ahead of the mules came into her view.

She heard the clatter of many hoofs. Quite a cavalcade was coming along the trail from the east. Out of the dust appeared a figure that Frances had learned to know well; and to tell the truth she was not sorry in her heart to see the smiling countenance of Pratt Sanderson.

"Hold on, Frances! Ye better listen to me a minute!" shouted the ex-cowboy behind her.

She gave him no attention. Molly sprang ahead and she met Pratt not far from the wagon. He stopped abruptly, as did the girl of the ranges.

Ratty M'Gill brought his own mount to a sudden halt within a few yards.

" Hello! " exclaimed Pratt. " What's the matter, Frances? "

" Why, Pratt! How came you and your friends to be riding this way? " returned the range girl.

She saw the red coat of the girl from Boston in the party passing the slowly moving wagon, and she was not at all sure that she was glad to see Pratt, after all!

But the young man had seen something suspicious in the manner in which Ratty M'Gill had been following Frances. The fellow now sat easily in his saddle at a little distance and rolled a cigarette, leering in the meantime at the ranch girl and her friend.

" What does that fellow want? " demanded Pratt again.

" Oh, don't mind him," said Frances, hurriedly. " He has been discharged from the Bar-T—— "

" That's the fellow you said made the steers stampede? " Pratt interrupted.

" Yes."

" Don't like his looks," the Amarillo young man said, frankly. " Glad we came up as we did."

" But you must go on with your friends, Pratt," said Frances, faintly.

"Goodness! there are enough of them, and the other fellows can get 'em all back to Mr. Bill Edwards' in time for supper," laughed Pratt. "I believe I'll go on with you. Where are you bound?"

"To Peckham's ranch," said Frances, faintly. "We shall stop there to-night."

The rest of the party passed, and Frances bowed to them. Sue Latrop looked at the ranch girl, curiously, but scarcely inclined her head. Frances felt that if she allowed Pratt to escort her she would make the Boston girl more of an enemy than she already felt her to be.

"We—we don't really need you, Pratt," said Frances. "Mack is all right—— "

"That fellow asleep on the wagon-seat? Lots of good *he* is as an escort," laughed Pratt.

"But I don't really need you," said the girl, weakly.

"Oh! don't be so offish!" cried the young man, more seriously. "Don't you suppose I'd be glad of the chance to ride with you for a way?"

"But your friends—— "

"You're a friend of mine," said Pratt, seriously. "I don't like the look of that Ratty M'Gill. I'm going to Peckham's with you."

What could Frances say? Ratty leered at her from his saddle. She knew he must be partly intoxicated, for he was very careless with his matches. He allowed a flaming splinter to fall to the trail, after he lit his cigarette, and, drunk or sober, a cattleman is seldom careless with fire on the plains.

It was mid-pasturage season and the ranges were already dry. A spark might at any time start a serious fire.

" We-ell," gasped Frances, at last. " I can't stop you from coming! "

" Of course not! " laughed Pratt, and quickly turned his grey pony to ride beside the pinto.

The wagon was now a long way ahead. They set off on a gallop to overtake it. But when Frances looked over her shoulder after a minute, Ratty M'Gill still remained on the trail, as though undecided whether to follow or not.

CHAPTER XVII

AN ACCIDENT

IT was not until later that Frances was disturbed by the thought that Pratt was suspected by her father of having a strong curiosity regarding the Spanish treasure chest.

"And here he has forced his company upon me," thought the girl. "What would father say, if he knew about it?"

But fortunately Captain Rugley was not at hand with his suspicions. Frances wished to believe the young man from Amarillo truly her friend; and on this ride toward Peckham's they became better acquainted than before.

That is, the girl of the ranges learned to know Pratt better. The young fellow talked more freely of himself, his mother, his circumstances.

"Just because I'm in a bank—the Merchants' and Drovers'—in Amarillo doesn't mean that I'm wealthy," laughed Pratt Sanderson. "They don't give me any great salary, and I couldn't afford this vacation if it wasn't for the extra work I did through the cattle-shipping season and the kindness of our president.

" Mother and I are all alone; and we haven't much money," pursued the young man, frankly. " Mother has a relative somewhere whom she suspects may be rich. He was a gold miner once. But I tell her there's no use thinking about rich relatives. They never seem to remember their poor kin. And I'm sure one can't blame them much.

" We have no reason to expect her half-brother to do anything for me. Guess I'll live and die a poor bank clerk. For, you know, if you haven't money to invest in bank stock yourself, or influential friends in the bank, one doesn't get very high in the clerical department of such an institution."

Frances listened to him with deeper interest than she was willing to show in her countenance. They rode along pleasantly together, and nothing marred the journey for a time.

Ratty had not followed them—as she was quite sure he would have done had not Pratt elected to become her escort. And as for the strange teamster who had turned into the trail ahead of them, his outfit had long since disappeared.

Once when Frances rode to the front of the covered wagon to speak to Mack, she saw that Pratt Sanderson lifted a corner of the canvas at the back and took a swift glance at what was within.

Why this curiosity? There was nothing to be seen in the wagon but the corded chest.

Frances sighed. She could credit Pratt with natural curiosity; but if her father had seen that act he would have been quite convinced that the young man from Amarillo was concerned in the attempt to get the treasure.

It was shortly thereafter that the trail grew rough. Some heavy wagon-train must have gone this way lately. The wheels had cut deep ruts and left holes in places into which the wheels of the Bar-T wagon slumped, rocking and wrenching the vehicle like a light boat caught in a cross-sea.

The wagon being nearly empty, however, Mack drove his mules at a reckless pace. He was desirous of reaching the Peckham ranch in good season for supper, and, to tell the truth, Frances, herself, was growing very anxious to get the day's ride over.

This haste was a mistake. Down went one forward wheel into a hole and crack went the axle. It was far too tough a stick of oak to break short off; but the crack yawned, finger-wide, and with a serious visage Mack climbed down, after quieting his mules.

The teamster's remarks were vividly picturesque, to say the least. Frances, too, was troubled by the delay. The sun was now low behind them

—disappearing below distant line of low, rolling hills.

Pratt got off his horse immediately and offered to help. And Mack needed his assistance.

"Lucky you was riding along with us, Mister," grumbled the teamster. "We got to jack up the old contraption, and splice the axle together. I got wire and pliers in the tool box and here's the wagon-jack."

He flung the implements out upon the ground. They set to work, Pratt removing his coat and doing his full share.

Meanwhile Frances sat on her pony quietly, occasionally riding around the stalled wagon so as to get a clear view of the plain all about. For a long time not a moving object crossed her line of vision.

"Who you looking for, Frances?" Pratt asked her, once.

"Oh, nobody," replied the girl.

"Do you expect that fellow is still trailing us?" he went on, curiously.

"No-o.   I think not."

"But he's on your mind, eh?" suggested Pratt, earnestly. "Just as well I came along with you," and he laughed.

"So Mack says," returned Frances, with an answering smile.

Was she expecting an attack? Would Ratty come back? Was the man, Pete, lurking in some hollow or buffalo wallow? She scanned the horizon from time to time and wondered.

The sun sank to sleep in a bed of gold and crimson. Pink and lavender tints flecked the cloud-coverlets he tucked about him.

It was full sunset and still the party was delayed. The mules stamped and rattled their harness. They were impatient to get on to their suppers and the freedom of the corral.

"We'll sure be too late for supper at Miz' Peckham's," grumbled Mack.

"Oh, you're only troubled about your eats," joked Pratt.

At that moment Frances uttered a little cry. Both Pratt and the teamster looked up at her inquiringly.

"What's the matter, Frances?" asked the young fellow.

"I—I thought I saw a light, away over there where the sun is going down."

"Plenty of light there, I should say," laughed Pratt. "The sun has left a field of glory behind him. Come on, now, Mr. Mack! Ready for this other wire?"

"Glory to Jehoshaphat!" grunted the teamster. "The world was made in a shorter time than it takes to bungle this mean, ornery job! I got a holler in me like the Cave of Winds."

" Hadn't we better take a bite here? " Frances demanded. " It will be bedtime when we reach the Peckhams."

" Wall, if you say so, Miss," said the teamster. " I kin eat as soon as you kin cook the stuff, sure! But I did hone for a mess of Miz' Peckham's flap-jacks."

Frances, well used to campwork, became immediately very busy. She ran for greasewood and such other fuel as could be found in the immediate vicinity, and started her fire.

It smoked and she got the strong smell of it in her nostrils, and it made her weep. Pratt, tugging and perspiring under the wagon-body, coughed over the smoke, too.

" Seems to me, Frances," he called, " you're filling the entire circumambient air with smoke—ker-chow!"

" Why! the wind isn't your way," said Frances, and she stood up to look curiously about again.

There seemed to be a lot of smoke. It was rolling in from the westward across the almost level plain. There was a deep rose glow behind it—a threatening illumination.

" Wow! " yelled Pratt.

He had just crawled out from beneath the

wagon and was rising to his feet. An object flew by him in the half-dusk, about shoulder-high, and so swiftly that he was startled. He stepped back into a gopher-hole, tripped, and fell full length.

" What in thunder was that? " he yelled, highly excited.

"A jack-rabbit," growled Mack. " And going some. Something scare't that critter, sure's you're bawn ! "

" Didn't you ever see a jack before, Pratt? " asked Frances, her tone a little queer, he thought.

" Not so close to," admitted the young fellow, as he scrambled to his feet. " Gracious! if he had hit me he'd have gone clear through me like a cannon-ball."

It was only Frances who had realized the unexpected peril. She had tried to keep her voice from shaking; but Mack noticed her tone.

"What's up, Miss? " he asked, getting to his legs, too.

" Fire! " gasped the range girl, clutching suddenly at Pratt's arm.

" You mean smoke," laughed Pratt. He saw her rubbing her eyes with her other hand.

But Mack had risen, facing the west. He uttered a funny little cluck in his throat and the laughing young fellow wheeled in wonder.

Along the horizon the glow was growing

rapidly. A tongue of yellow flame shot high in the air. A long dead, thoroughly seasoned tree, standing at the forks of the trail, had caught fire and the flame flared forth from its top like a banner.

The prairie was afire!

" Glory to Jehoshaphat! " groaned Mack Hinkman, again. " Who done that? "

" Goodness! " gasped Pratt, quite horror-stricken.

Frances gathered up the cooking implements and flung them into the wagon. She had hobbled Molly and the grey pony; now she ran for them.

" Got that axle fixed, Mack? " she shouted over her shoulder.

" Not for no rough traveling, I tell ye sure, Miss Frances! " complained the teamster. " That was a bad crack. Have to wait to fix it proper at Peckham's." Then he added, *sotto voce:* " If we get the blamed thing there at all."

" Don't say that, man! " gasped Pratt Sanderson. " Surely there's not much danger? "

" This here spot will be scorched like an over-done flapjack in half an hour," declared Hinkman. " We got to git! "

Frances heard him, distant as she was.

" Oh, Mack! you know we can't reach the river in half an hour, even if we travel express speed."

" Well! what we goin' ter do then? " demanded the teamster. " Stay here and fry? "

Pratt was impressed suddenly with the thought that they were both leaning on the advice and leadership of the girl! He was inexperienced, himself; and the teamster seemed quite as helpless.

A pair of coyotes, too frightened by the fire to be afraid of their natural enemy, man, shot by in the dusk—two dim, grey shapes.

Frances released Molly and the grey pony from their hobbles. She leaped upon the back of the pinto and dragged the grey after by his bridle-reins. She was back at the stalled wagon in a few moments.

Already the flames could be seen along the western horizon as far as the unaided eye could see anything, leaping under the pall of rising smoke. The fire was miles away, it was true; but its ominous appearance affrighted even Pratt Sanderson, who knew so little about such peril.

Mack was fastening straps and hooking up traces; they had not dared leave the mules hitched to the wagon while they were engaged in its repair.

" Come on! get a hustle on you, Mister! " exclaimed the teamster. " We got to light out o' here right sudden! "

CHAPTER XVIII

THE WAVE OF FLAME

PRATT was pale, as could be seen where his face was not smudged with earth and axle-grease. He came and accepted his pony's bridle from Frances' hand.

" What shall we do? " he asked, trying to keep his voice steady.

It was plain that the teamster had little idea of what was wise or best to do. The young fellow turned to Frances of the ranges quite as a matter of course. Evidently, she knew so much more about the perilous circumstances than he did that Pratt was not ashamed to take Frances' commands.

" This is goin' to be a hot corner," the teamster drawled again; but Pratt waited for the girl to speak.

" Are you frightened, Pratt? " she asked, suddenly, looking down at him from her saddle, and smiling rather wistfully.

" Not yet," said the young fellow. " I expect I shall be if it is very terrible."

"But you don't expect me to be scared?" asked Frances, still gravely.

"I don't think it is your nature to show apprehension," returned he.

"I'm not like other girls, you mean. That girl from Boston, for instance?" Frances said, looking away at the line of fire again. "Well!" and she sighed. "I am not, I suppose. With daddy I've been up against just such danger as this before. You never saw a prairie fire, Pratt?"

"No, ma'am!" exclaimed Pratt. "I never did."

"The grass and greasewood are just right for it now. Mack is correct," the girl went on. "This will be a hot corner."

"And that mighty quick!" cried Mack.

"But you don't propose to stay here?" gasped Pratt.

"Not much! Hold your mules, Mack," she called to the grumbling teamster. "I'm going to make a flare."

"Better do somethin' mighty suddent, Miss," growled the man.

She spurred Molly up to the wagon-seat and there seized one of the blankets.

"Got a sharp knife, Pratt?" she asked, shaking out the folds of the blanket.

"Yes."

" Slit this blanket, then—lengthwise. Halve it,"
urged Frances. " And be quick."

" That's right, Miss Frances ! " called the teamster. " Set a backfire both sides of the trail. We
got to save ourselves. Be sure ye run it a mile or
more."

" Do you mean to burn the prairie ahead of
us ? " panted Pratt.

" Yes. We'll have to. I hope nobody will be
hurt. But the way that fire is coming back there,"
said Frances, firmly, " the flames will be ten feet
high when they get here."

" You don't mean it ! "

" Yes. You'll see. Pray we may get a burned-
over area before us in time to escape. The flames
will leap a couple of hundred feet or more before
the supply of gas—or whatever it is that burns so
high above the ground—expires. The breath of
that flame will scorch us to cinders if it reaches us.
It will kill and char a big steer in a few seconds.
Oh, it is a serious situation we're in, Pratt ! "

" Can't we keep ahead of it ? " demanded the
young man, anxiously.

" Not for long," replied Frances, with convic-
tion. " I've seen more than one such fire, as I
tell you. There ! Take this rawhide."

The ranchman's daughter was not idle while she
talked. She showed him how to knot the length of

rawhide which she had produced from under the
wagon-seat to one end of his share of the blanket.
Her own fingers were busy with the other half
meanwhile.

"Into your saddle now, Pratt. Take the
right-hand side of the trail. Ride as fast as you
can toward the river when I give the word. Go a
mile, at least."

The ponies were urged close to the campfire
and he followed Frances' example when she flung
the tail of her piece of blanket into the blaze. The
blankets caught fire and began to smoulder and
smoke. There was enough cotton mixed with the
wool to cause it to catch fire quickly.

"All right! We're off!" shouted Frances, and
spurred her pinto in the opposite direction. Immediately the smouldering blanket-stuff was blown
into a live flame. Wherever it touched the dry
grass and clumps of low brush fire started like
magic.

Immediately Pratt reproduced her work on the
other side of the trail. At right angles with the
beaten path, they fled across the prairie, leaving
little fires in their wake that spread and spread,
rising higher and higher, and soon roaring into
quenchless conflagrations.

These patches of fire soon joined and increased
to a wider and wider swath of flame. The fire

traveled slowly westward, but rushed eastward, propelled by the wind.

Wider and wider grew the sea of flame set by the burning blankets. Like Frances, Pratt kept his mount at a fast lope—the speediest pace of the trained cow-pony—nor did he stop until the blanket was consumed to the rawhide knot.

Then he wheeled his mount to look back. He could see nothing but flames and smoke at first. He did not know how far Frances had succeeded in traveling with her " flare "; but he was quite sure that he had come more than a mile from the wagon-trail.

He could soon see a broadening patch of burned-over prairie in the midst of the swirling flames and smoke. His pony snorted, and backed away from the approach-fire; but Pratt wheeled the grey around to the westward, and where the flames merely crept and sputtered through the grease-wood and against the wind, he spurred his mount to leap over the line of fire.

The earth was hot, and every time the pony set a hoof down smoke or sparks flew upward; but Pratt had to get back to the trail. With the quirt he forced on the snorting grey, and finally reached a place where the fire had completely passed and the ground was cooler.

Ashes flew in clouds about him; the smoke from

the west drove in a thick mass between him and the darkened sky. Only the glare of the roaring fire revealed objects and landmarks.

The backfire had burned for many yards westward, to meet the threatening wave of flame flying on the wings of the wind. To the east, the line of flame Pratt and Frances had set was rising higher and higher.

He saw the wagon standing in the midst of the smoke, Mack Hinkman holding the snorting, kicking mules with difficulty, while a wild little figure on a pony galloped back from the other side of the trail.

·"All right, Pratt?" shrieked Frances. "Get up, Mack; we've no time to lose!"

The teamster let the mules go. Yet he dared not let them take their own gait. The thought of that cracked axle disturbed him.

The wagon led, however, through the smoke and dust; the two ponies fell in behind upon the trail. Frances and Pratt looked at each other. The young man was serious enough; but the girl was smiling.

Something she had said a little while before kept returning to Pratt's mind. He was thinking of what would have happened had Sue Latrop, the girl from Boston, been here instead of Frances.

"Goodness!" Pratt told himself. "They are

out of two different worlds; that's sure! And I'm an awful tenderfoot, just as Mrs. Bill Edwards says."

"What do you think of it?" asked Frances, raising her voice to make it heard above the roar of the fire and the rumble of the wagon ahead of them.

"I'm scared—right down scared!" admitted Pratt Sanderson.

"Well, so was I," she admitted. "But the worst is over now. We'll reach the river and ford it, and so put the fire all behind us. The flames won't leap the river, that's sure."

The heat from the prairie fire was most oppressive. Over their heads the hot smoke swirled, shutting out all sight of the stars. Now and then a clump of brush beside the trail broke into flame again, fanned by the wind, and the ponies snorted and leaped aside.

Suddenly Mack was heard yelling at the mules and trying to pull them down to something milder than a wild gallop. Frances and Pratt spurred their ponies out upon the burned ground in order to see ahead.

Something loomed up on the trail—something that smoked and flamed like a big bonfire.

"What can it be?" gasped Pratt, riding knee to knee with the range girl.

"Not a house.   There isn't one along here," she returned.

"Some old-timer got caught!" yelled the teamster, looking back at the two pony-riders.   "Hope he saved his skin."

"A wagoner!" cried Frances, startled.

"He cut his stock loose, of course," yelled Mack Hinkman.

But when they reached the burning wagon they saw that this was not altogether true.   One horse lay, charred, in the harness.   The wagon had been empty.   The driver of it had evidently cut his other horse loose and ridden away on its back to save himself.

"And why didn't he free this poor creature?" demanded Pratt.   "How cruel!"

"He was scare't," said Mack, pulling his mules out of the trail so as to drive around the burning wagon.   "Or mebbe the hawse fell.   Like enough that's it."

Frances said nothing more.   She was wondering if this abandoned wagon was the one she had seen turn into the trail from Cottonwood Bottom early in the day?   And who was its driver?

They went on, puzzled by this incident.   At least, Frances and Pratt were puzzled by it.

"We may see the fellow at the ford," Frances said.   "Too bad he lost his outfit."

" He didn't have anything in that wagon," said Pratt. " It was as empty as your own."

Frances looked at him curiously. She remembered that the young man from Amarillo had taken a peep into the Bar-T wagon when he joined them on the trail. He must have seen the heavy chest; and now he ignored it.

On and on they rode. The smoke made the ride very unpleasant, even if the flames were now at a distance. Behind them the glare of the fire decreased; but to north and south the wall of flame, at a distance of several miles, rushed on and passed the riders on the trail.

The trees along the river's brink came into view, outlined in many places by red and yellow flames. The fire would do a deal of damage along here, for even the greenest trees would be badly scorched.

The mules had run themselves pretty much out of breath and finally reduced their pace; but the wagon still led the procession when it reached the high bank.

The water in the river was very low; the trail descended the bank on a slant, and Mack put on the brakes and allowed the sure-footed mules to take their own course to the ford.

With hanging heads and heaving flanks, the two cow-ponies followed. Frances and Pratt were

scorched, and smutted from head to foot; and
their throats were parched, too.

"I hope I'll never have to take such another
ride," admitted the young man from Amarillo.
"Adventure is all right, Frances; but clerking in a
bank doesn't prepare one for such a strenuous
life."

"I think you are game, Pratt," she said, frankly.
"I can see that Mack, even, thinks you are pretty
good—for a tenderfoot."

The wagon went into the water at that moment.
Mack yelled to the mules to stop. The wagon
was hub deep in the stream and he loosened the
reins so that the animals might plunge their noses
into the flood. Molly and the grey quickly put
down their heads, too.

Above the little group the flames crackled in a
dead-limbed tree, lighting the ford like a huge
torch. Above the flare of the thick canopy of the
smoke spread out, completely overcasting the
river.

Suddenly Frances laid her hand upon Pratt's
arm. She pointed with her quirt into a bushy
tree on the opposite bank.

"Look over there!" she exclaimed, in a low
tone.

Almost as she spoke there sounded the sharp
crack of a rifle, and a ball passed through the top

of the wagon, so near that it made the ponies jump.

"Put up your hands—all three of you folks down there!" commanded an angry voice. "The magazine of this rifle is plumb full and I can shoot straight. D'ye get me? Hands up!"

"My goodness!" gasped Pratt Sanderson.

What Mack Hinkman said was muffled in his own beard; but his hands shot upward as he sat on the wagon-seat.

Frances said nothing; her heart jumped—and then pumped faster. She recognized the drawling voice of the man in the tree, although she could not see his face clearly in the firelight.

It was Pete—Ratty M'Gill's acquaintance—the man who had been orderly at the Bylittle Soldiers' Home, and who had come all the way to the Panhandle to try to secure the treasure in the old Spanish chest.

Perhaps Frances had half expected some such incident as this to punctuate her journey to Amarillo. Nevertheless, the reckless tone of the man, and the way he used his rifle, troubled her.

"Put your hands up!" she murmured to Pratt. "Do just what he tells you. He may be wicked and foolish enough to fire again."

OVER THEIR HEADS THE HOT SMOKE SWIRLED.

Page 166.

CHAPTER XIX

MOST ASTONISHING!

"THE man must be crazy!" murmured the young bank clerk.

"All the more reason why we should be careful to obey him," Frances said.

Yet she was not unmindful of the peril Pratt pointed out. Only, in Frances' case, she had been brought up among men who carried guns habitually, and the sound of a rifle shot did not startle her as it did the young man.

"Look yere, Mr. Hold-up Man!" yelled Mack Hinkman, when his amazement let him speak. "Ain't you headed in the wrong way? We ain't comin' from town with a load. Why, man! we're only jest goin' to town. Why didn't you wait till we was comin' back before springin' this mine on us?"

"Keep still there," commanded Pete, from the tree. "Drive on through the river, and up on this bank, and then stop! You hear?"

"I'd hear ye, I reckon, if I was plumb deef," complained Mack. "That rifle you handle so permiscuous speaks mighty plain."

"Let them on hossback mind it, too," added the man in the tree. "I got an eye on 'em."

"Easy, Mister," urged Mack, as he picked up the reins again. "One o' them is a young lady. You're a gent, I take it, as wouldn't frighten no female."

"Stow that!" advised Pete, with vigor. "Come out o' there!"

Mack started the mules, and they dragged the wagon creakingly up the bank. Frances and Pratt rode meekly in its wake. The man in the tree had selected his station with good judgment. When Mack halted his four mules, and Frances and Pratt obeyed a commanding gesture to stop at the water's edge, all three were splendid targets for the man behind the rifle.

"Ride up to that wagon, young fellow," commanded Pete. "Rip open that canvas. That's right. Roll off your horse and climb inside; but don't you go out of sight. If you do I'll make that canvas cover a sieve in about one minute. Get me?"

Pratt nodded. He could not help himself. He gave an appealing glance toward Frances. She nodded.

"Don't be foolish, Pratt," she whispered. "Do what he tells you to do."

Thus encouraged, the young fellow obeyed the

mandate of the man who had stopped them on the trail. He had read of highwaymen and hold-ups; but he had believed that such things had gone out of fashion with the coming of farmers into the Panhandle, the building up of the frequent settlements, and the extension of the railroad lines.

Pratt's heart was warmed by the girl's evident desire that he should not run into danger. The outlaw in the tree was after the chest hidden in the wagon; but Frances put his safety above the value of the treasure chest.

" Heave that chist out of the end of the wagon, and be quick about it! " was the expected order from the desperado. " And don't try anything funny, young fellow."

Pratt was in no mood to be " funny." He hesitated just a moment. But Frances exclaimed:

" Do as he says! Don't wait! "

So out rolled the chest. Mack was grumbling to himself on the front seat; but if he was armed he did not consider it wise to use any weapon. The man with the rifle had everything his own way.

" Now, drive on! " commanded the latter individual. " I've got no use for any of you folks here, and you'll be wise if you keep right on moving till you get to that Peckham ranch. Git now! "

"All right, old-timer," grunted Mack. "Don't be so short-tempered about it."

He let the mules go and they scrambled up the bank, drawing the wagon after them. The chest lay on the river's edge. Pratt Sanderson had climbed upon his pony again.

"You two git, also," growled the man in the tree. "I got all I want of ye."

Pratt groaned aloud as he urged the grey pony after Molly.

"What will your father say, Frances?" he muttered.

"I don't know," returned the girl, honestly.

"I'm going to ride ahead to the Peckham ranch and rouse them. That fellow can't get away with that heavy chest on horseback."

"I'll go with you," returned the ranchman's daughter. "That rascal should be apprehended and punished. We have about chased such people out of this section of the country."

"Goodness! you take it calmly, Frances," exclaimed Pratt. "Doesn't *anything* ruffle you?"

She laughed shortly, and made no further remark. They rode on swiftly and within the hour saw the lights of Peckham's ranch-house.

Their arrival brought the family to the door, as well as half a dozen punchers up from the bunk-house. The fire had excited everybody and kept them out of bed, although there was no danger of the conflagration's jumping the river.

"Why, Miss Frances!" cried the ranchman's wife, who was a fleshy and notoriously good-natured woman, the soul of Western hospitality. "Why, Miss Frances! if you ain't a cure for sore eyes! Do 'light and come in—and yer friend, too.

"My goodness me! ye don't mean to say you've been through that fire? That is awful! Come right on in, do!"

But what Frances and Pratt had to tell about their adventure at the ford excited the Peckhams and their hands much more than the fire.

"John Peckham!" commanded the fleshy lady, who was really the leading spirit at the ranch. "You take a bunch of the boys and ride right after that rascal. My mercy! are folks goin' to be held up on this trail and robbed just as though we had no law and order? It's disgraceful!"

Then she turned her mind to another idea. "Miss Frances!" she exclaimed. "What was in that trunk? Must have been something valuable, eh?"

"I was taking it to the Amarillo bank, to put it in the safe deposit vaults," Frances answered, dodging the direct question.

"'Twarn't full of money?" shrieked Mrs. Peckham.

"Why, no!" laughed Frances. "We're not as rich as all that, you know."

"Well," sighed the good, if curious, woman, "I reckon there was 'nough sight more valuables in the trunk than Captain Dan Rugley wants to lose. Hurry up, there, John Peckham!" she shouted after her husband. "Git after that fellow before he has a chance to break open the trunk."

"I'm going to get a fresh horse and ride back with them," Pratt Sanderson told Frances. "And we'll get that chest, don't you fear."

"You'd better remain here and have your night's rest," advised the girl, wonderfully calm, it would seem. "Let Mr. Peckham and his men catch that bad fellow."

"And me sit here idle?" cried Pratt. "Not much!"

She saw him start for the corral, and suddenly showed emotion. "Oh, Pratt!" she cried, weakly.

The young man did not hear her. Should she shout louder for him? She paled and then grew rosy red. Should she run after him? Should she tell him the truth about that chest?

"Do come in the house, Miss Frances," urged Mrs. Peckham. And the girl from the Bar-T obeyed her and allowed Pratt to go.

"You must sure be done up," said Mrs. Peck-

ham, bustling about.   "I'll make you a cup of
tea."

"Thank you," said Frances.   She listened for
the posse to start, and knew that, when they
dashed away, Pratt Sanderson was with them.

Mack Hinkman arrived with the double mule
team soon after.   He said the crowd had gone by
him "on the jump."

"I 'low they'll ketch that feller that stole your
chist, Miss Frances, 'bout the time two Sundays
come together in the week," he declared.   "He's
had plenty of time to make himself scarce."

"But the trunk?" cried Mrs. Peckham.   "That
was some heavy, wasn't it?"

"Aw, he had a wagon handy.   He wouldn't
have tried to take the chist if he hadn't.   Don't
you say so, Miss Frances?" said the teamster.

"I don't know," said the girl, and she spoke
wearily.   Indeed, she had suddenly become tired of
hearing the robbery discussed.

"Don't trouble the poor girl," urged Mrs.
Peckham.   "She's all done up.   We'll know all
about it when John Peckham gets back.   You
wanter go to bed, honey?"

Frances was glad to retire.   Not alone was she
weary, but she wished to escape any further discus-
sion of the incident at the ford.

Mrs. Peckham showed her to the room she was

to occupy. Mack would remain up to repair properly the cracked axle of the wagon.

For, whether the chest was recovered or not, Frances proposed to go right on in the morning to Amarillo.

She did not awaken when Mr. Peckham and his men returned; but Frances was up at daybreak and came into the kitchen for breakfast. Mrs. Peckham was bustling about just as she had been the night before when the girl from the Bar-T retired.

"Hard luck, Miss Frances!" the good lady cried. "Them men ain't worth more'n two bits a dozen, when it comes to sending 'em out on a trail. They never got your trunk for you at all!"

"And they did not catch the man who stopped us at the ford?"

"Of course not. John Peckham never could catch anything but a cold."

"But where could he have gone—that man, I mean?" queried Frances.

"Give it up! One party went up stream and t'other down. Your friend, Mr. Sanderson, went with the first party."

"Oh, yes," Frances commented. "That would be on his way to the Edwards ranch where he is staying."

"Well, mebbe. They say he was mighty anxious

to find your trunk. He's an awful nice young man—— "

" Where's Mack? " asked Frances, endeavoring to stem the tide of the lady's speech.

" He's a-getting the team ready, Frances. He's done had his breakfast. And I never did see a man with such a holler to fill with flapjacks. He eat seventeen."

" Mack's appetite is notorious at the ranch," admitted Frances, glad Mrs. Peckham had finally switched from the subject of the lost chest.

" He was telling me about that burned wagon you passed on the trail. Can't for the life of me think who it could belong to," said Mrs. Peckham.

" We thought once that Mr. Bob Ellis was ahead of us on the trail," said Frances.

" He'd have come right on here," declared the ranchman's wife. " No. 'Twarn't Bob."

" Then I thought it might have belonged to that man who stopped us," suggested Frances.

" If that's so, I reckon he got square for his loss, didn't he? " cried the lady. " I reckon that chest was filled with valuables, eh? "

Fortunately, Frances had swallowed her coffee and the mule team rattled to the door.

" I must hurry! " the girl cried, jumping up. " Many, many thanks, dear Mrs. Peckham! " and she kissed the good woman and so got out of the house without having to answer any further questions.

She sprang into Molly's saddle and Mack cracked his whip over the mules.

" Mebbe we'll have good news for you when you come back, Frances! " called the ranchwoman, quite filling the door with her ample person as she watched the Bar-T wagon, and the girl herself, take the trail for Amarillo.

Mack Hinkman was quite wrought up over the adventure of the previous evening.

" That young Pratt Sanderson is some smart boy—believe me ! " he said to Frances, who elected to ride within earshot of the wagon-seat for the first mile or two.

" How is that ? " she asked, curiously.

" They tell me it was him found the place where the chest had been put aboard that punt."

" What punt ? "

" The boat the feller escaped in with the chest," said Mack.

" Then he wasn't the man whose wagon and one horse was burned ? " queried Frances.

" Don't know.   Mebbe.   But that's no difference.   This old punt has been hid down there below the ford since last duck-shooting season. Maybe he knowed 'twas there; maybe he didn't. Howsomever, he found the boat and brought it up

to the ford.   Into the boat he tumbled the chest.
There was the marks on the bank.   John Peckham
told me himself."

" And Pratt found the trail? "

" That's what he did.   Smart boy!   The rest of
'em was up a stump when they didn't find the chest
knocked to pieces.   The hold-up gent didn't even
stop to open it."

" He expected we'd set somebody on his trail,"
Frances said, reflectively.

" In   course.   Two   parties.   One   went   up
stream and t'other down."

" So Mrs. Peckham just told me."

" Wal!" said Mack.   " Mebbe one of 'em will
ketch the varmint! "

But Frances made no further comment.   She
rode on in silence, her mind vastly troubled.   And
mostly her thought connected Pratt Sanderson
with the disappearance of the chest.

Why had the young fellow been so sure that the
robber had gone up stream instead of down?   It
did not seem reasonable that the man would have
tried to stem the current in the heavy punt—nor
was the chest a light weight.

It puzzled Frances—indeed, it made her suspicious.   She was anxious to learn whether the
man who had stolen the chest had gone up, or
down, the river.

CHAPTER XX

FRANCES warned Mack to say nothing about the hold-up at the ford. That was certainly laying no cross on the teamster's shoulders, for he was not generally garrulous.

They put up at the hotel that night and Frances did her errands in Amarillo the next day without being disturbed by awkward questions regarding their adventure.

Certainly, she was not obliged to go to the bank under the present circumstances, for there was no chest now to put in the safe-keeping of that institution.

Nor did Frances Rugley have many friends in the breezy, Western city with whom she might spend her time. Two years make many changes in such a fast-growing community. She was not sure that she would be able to find many of the girls with whom she had gone to high school.

And she was, too, in haste to return to the Bar-T. Although she had left her father better, she worried much about him. Naturally, too, she wished to get back and report to him the adventures which had marked her journey to Amarillo.

She would have been glad to escape stopping at the Peckham ranch over the third night; but she could not get beyond that point—the wagon now being heavily laden; nor did she wish to remain out on the range at night without a shelter tent.

The hold-up at the ford naturally made Frances feel somewhat timid, too. Mack was not armed, and she had only the revolver that she usually carried in her saddle holster and wouldn't have thought of defending herself with it from any human being.

So she rode ahead when it became dark, and reached the Peckham ranch at supper time, finding both a warm welcome and much news awaiting her.

" Glad to see ye back again, Frances," declared Mrs. Peckham. " We done been talking about you and your hold-up most of the time since you went to Amarillo. Beats all how little it does take to set folks' tongues wagging in the country. Ain't it so?

" Well! that feller got clean away. And he took chest and all. Them fellers that went down stream found the old punt. But they never found no place where he'd shifted the trunk ashore. And it must have been heavy, Frances? "

" Oh, yes! "

"Must have been a sight of valuables in it," repeated Mrs. Peckham.

"What about those who went up stream?" asked Frances, quickly.

"There! your friend, Mr. Sanderson, didn't come back. He went on to Mr. Bill Edwards' place, so he said. He axed would you lead his grey pony on behind your wagon to the Bar-T. Said he'd come after it there."

"Yes; of course," returned Frances. "But didn't he find any trace of the robber up stream?"

"How could they, Miss Frances, if the boat went down?" demanded Mrs. Peckham. "Of course not."

It was true. Frances worried about this. Pratt Sanderson had insisted upon leading a part of the searchers in exactly the opposite direction to that in which common sense should have told him the robber had gone with the chest.

"Of course he would never have tried to pole against the current," Frances told herself. "I am afraid daddy will consider that significant."

She did not attempt to keep the story from Captain Dan Rugley when she got back home on the fourth evening.

"Smart girl!" the old ranchman said, when she told him of the make-believe treasure chest she had carted halfway to Amarillo, burlapped, corded, and tagged as though for deposit in the city bank for safe-keeping.

"Smart girl!" he repeated. "Fooled 'em good. But maybe you were reckless, Frances—just a wee mite reckless."

"I had no intention of trying to defend the chest, or of letting Mack," she told him.

"And how about that Pratt boy who you say went along with you?" queried the Captain, his brows suddenly coming together.

"Well, Daddy! He insisted upon going with me because Ratty bothered me," said Frances, in haste.

"Humph! Mack could break that M'Gill in two if the foolish fellow became really fresh with you. Now! I don't want to say anything to hurt your feelings, Frances; but it does seem to me that this Pratt Sanderson was too handy when that hold-up man got the chest."

It was just as the girl feared. She bit her lip and said nothing. She did not see what there was to say in Pratt's defense. Besides, in her secret heart she, too, was troubled about the young fellow from Amarillo.

She wondered what the robber at the ford thought about it when he got the old trunk open and found in it nothing but some junk and rubbish she had found in the attic of the ranch-house. At least, she had managed to draw the attention of the dishonest orderly from the Bylittle Soldiers' Home from the real Spanish treasure chest for several days.

Before he could make any further attempt against the peace of mind of her father and herself, Frances hoped Mr. Lonergan would have arrived at the Bar-T and the responsibility for the safety of the treasure would be lifted from their shoulders.

At any rate, the mysterious treasure would be divided and disposed of. When Pete knew that the Spanish treasure chest was opened and the valuables divided, he might lose hope of gaining possession of the wealth he coveted.

A telegram had come while Frances was absent from the chaplain of the Soldiers' Home, stating that Mr. Lonergan would start for the Panhandle in a week, if all went well with him.

Captain Rugley was as eager as a boy for his old partner's appearance.

" And I've been wishing all these years," he said, " while you were growing up, Frances, to dress you up in a lot of this fancy jewelry. It would have been for your mother if she had lived."

" But you don't want me to look like a South Sea Island princess, do you, Daddy? " Frances said, laughing. " I can see that the belt and brace-

let I wore the night Pratt stopped here rather
startled him.   He's used to seeing ladies dressed
up, in Amarillo, too."

"Pooh! In the cities women are ablaze with
jewels.   Your mother and I went to Chicago once,
and we went to the opera.   Say! that was a show!

" Let me tell you, there are things in that chest
that will outshine anything in the line of ornaments
that that Pratt Sanderson—or any other Amarillo
person—ever saw."

The girl was quite sure that this desire on her
father's part of arraying her in the gaudy jewels
from the old chest was bound to make her the
laughing-stock of the people who were coming out
from Amarillo to see the Pageant of the Panhandle.

But what could she do about it? His wish was
fathered by his love for her. She must wear the
gems to please him, for Frances would never do
anything to hurt his feelings, for the world.

A good many of their friends, of course—people
like good Mrs. Peckham—would never realize the
incongruity of a girl being bedecked like a barbarian princess. But Frances wondered what the
girl from Boston would say to Pratt Sanderson
about it, if she chanced to see Frances so adorned?

She had an opportunity of seeing something
more of the Boston girl shortly, for in a day or

two Pratt Sanderson came over for the grey pony he had left at the Peckham ranch, and Frances had led back to the Bar-T for him.

And with Pratt trailed along Mrs. Bill Edwards and the visitors whom Frances had met twice before.

By this time Captain Dan Rugley was able to hobble out upon the veranda, and was sitting there in his old, straight-backed chair when the cavalcade rode up. He hailed Mrs. Edwards, and welcomed her and her young friends as heartily as it was his nature so to do.

" Come in, all of you! " he shouted. " Ming will bring out a pitcher of something cool to drink in a minute; and San Soo can throw together a luncheon that'll keep you from starving to death before you get back to Bill's place."

He would not listen to refusals. The Mexican boys took the ponies away and a round dozen of visitors settled themselves—like a covey of prairie chickens—about the huge porch.

Frances welcomed everybody quietly, but with a smile. She instructed Ming to set tables in the inner court of the *hacienda*, as it would be both cool and shady there on this hot noontide.

She noticed that Sue Latrop scarcely bowed to her, and immediately set about chattering to two or three of her companions. Frances did not

mind for herself; but she saw that the girl from
Boston seemed amused by Captain Rugley's talk,
and was not well-bred enough to conceal her
amusement.

The old ranchman was not dull in any particular, however; before long he found an opportunity
to say to his daughter:

"Who's the girl in the fancy fixin's? That red
coat's got style to it, I reckon?"

"If you like the style," laughed Frances, smiling tenderly at him.

"You don't? And I see she doesn't cotton
much to you, Frances. What's the matter?"

"She's Eastern," explained Frances, briefly.
"I imagine she thinks I am crude."

"'Crude'? What's 'crude'?" demanded Captain Dan Rugley. "That isn't anything very bad,
is it, Frances?" and his eyes twinkled.

"Can't be anything much worse, Daddy," she
whispered, "if you are all 'fed up,' as the boys
say, on 'culchaw'!"

He chuckled at that, and began to eye Sue
Latrop with more interest. When the shuffle-
footed Ming called them to luncheon, he kept close
to the girl from Boston, and sat with her and Mrs.
Bill Edwards at one of the small tables.

"I reckon you're not used to this sort of slap-
dash eating, Miss?" suggested Captain Rugley,

with perfect gravity, as he saw Sue casting doubtful glances about the inner garden.

The fountain was playing, the trees rustled
softly overhead, a little breeze played in some
mysterious way over the court, and from the distance came the tinkle of some Mexican mandolins,
for Frances had hidden José and his brother in one
of the shadowy rooms.

"Oh, it's quite *al fresco,* don't you know,"
drawled Sue. "Altogether novel and chawming
—isn't it, Mrs. Edwards?"

The neighboring rancher's wife had originally come from the East herself; but she had lived
long enough in the Panhandle to have quite rubbed
off the veneer of that " culchaw " of which Sue was
an exponent.

"The Bar-T is the show place of the Panhandle," she said, promptly. "We are rather
proud of it—all of us ranchers."

"Indeed? I had no idea!" cooed the girl from
Boston. "And I thought all you ranch folk had
your wealth in cattle, and re'lly had no time for
much social exchange."

"Oh!" exclaimed the Captain, "when we have
folks come to see us we manage to treat 'em with
our best."

Sue was obliged to note that the service and the
napery were dainty, and what she had seen of the

furnishings of the darkened hall amazed her—as it had Pratt on his first visit.   The food was, of course, good and well prepared, for San Soo was " A Number One, topside " cook, as he would have himself expressed it in pigeon English.

Yet Sue could not satisfy herself that these " cattle people " were really worthy of her attention. Had she not been with Mrs. Edwards she would have made open fun of the old Captain and his daughter.

Frances of the ranges looked a good deal like a girl on a moving picture screen.   She was in her riding dress, short skirt, high gaiters, tight-fitting jacket, and with her hair in plaits.

The Captain looked as though he had never worn anything but the loose alpaca coat he now had on, with the carpet-slippers upon his blue-stockinged feet.

" Re'lly! " Sue whispered to Pratt, as they all arose to return to the front of the house, " they are quite too impossible, aren't they? "

" Who? " asked Pratt, with narrowing gaze.

" Why—er—this cowgirl and her father."

" I only see that they are very hospitable," the young man said, pointedly, and he kept away from the Boston girl for the remainder of their visit to the Bar-T ranch-house.

CHAPTER XXI

IN THE HANDS OF THE ENEMY

SILENT SAM had reported some jack-rabbits on one of the southern ranges, and the Captain thought it would interest the party from the Edwards ranch to come over the next day and help run them.

Jack-rabbits have become such a nuisance in certain parts of the West of late years that a price has been set upon their heads, and the farmers and ranchmen often organize big drives to clear the ranges of the pests.

This was only a small drive on the Bar-T; but Captain Rugley had several good dogs, and the occasion was an interesting one—for everybody but the jacks.

Of course, the old ranchman could not go; but Frances and Sam were at Cottonwood Bottom soon after sunrise, waiting for the party from Mr. Bill Edwards' ranch.

José Reposa had the dogs in leash—two long-legged, sharp-nosed, mouse-colored creatures, more than half greyhound, but with enough mongrel in their make-up to make them bite when they ran down the long-eared pests that they were trained to drive.

The branch of the river that ran through Cottonwood Bottom was too shallow—at least, at this season—to float even a punt. Frances gazed down the wooded and winding hollow and asked Silent Sam a question:

" Do you know of any place along the river where a man might hide out—that fellow who stopped us at the ford the other evening, for instance ? "

" There's a right smart patch of small growth down below Bill Edwards' line," said Sam. " The boys from Peckham's, with that Pratt Sanderson, didn't more'n skirt that rubbish, I reckon, by what Mack said," Sam observed. " Mebbe that hombre might have laid up there for a while."

" Before or after he robbed us ? " Frances asked quietly.

" Wall, now ! " ejaculated Sam. " If he took that chest aboard the punt, and the punt was found below the ford—— "

" You know, Sam," said the girl, thoughtfully, " that he might have poled up stream a way, put the chest ashore, and then let the punt drift down."

" Reckon that's so," grunted the foreman.

He said no more, and neither did Frances. But

the brief dialogue gave the girl food for thought, and her mind was quite full of the idea when the crowd from the Edwards ranch came into view.

The boys were armed with light rifles or shot-guns, and even some of the girls were armed, as well as Mrs. Edwards herself.

But Sue Latrop had never fired a gun in her life, and she professed to be not much interested in this hunt.

" Oh, I've fox-hunted several times.   That is real sport!   But we don't shoot foxes.   The dogs kill them—if there re'lly *is* a fox."

" Humph! " asked one of the local boys, with wonder, " what do the dogs follow, if there's no fox?   What scent do they trail, I mean? "

" Oh," said Sue, " a man rides ahead dragging an aniseed bag.   Some dogs are trained to fol-low that scent and nothing else.   It's very exciting, I assure you."

" Well! what do you know about that? " gasped the questioner.

" Say! was this around Boston? " asked Pratt, his eyes twinkling.

" Oh, yes.   There is a fine pack of hounds at Arlington," drawled Sue.

" Sho! " chuckled Pratt.   " I should think they'd teach the dogs around Boston to follow the trail of a bean-bag.   Wouldn't it be easier? "

"Oh, dear me!" exclaimed Miss Latrop. "Don't you think you are witty? And look at those dogs!"

"What's the matter with them?" asked one of the girls.

"Why, they are all limbs! What perfectly spidery-looking animals! Did you ever——"

"You wait a bit," laughed Mrs. Edwards. "Those long-legged dogs are just what we need hunting the jacks. And if we didn't have guns, at that, there would be few of the rabbits caught. All ready, Sam Harding?"

"Jest when Miss Frances says the word, Ma'am," returned the foreman, coolly.

"Of course! Frances is mistress of the hunt," said the ranchman's wife, good-naturedly.

Sue Latrop had been coaxed to leave her Eastern-bred horse behind on this occasion, and was upon one of the ponies broken to side-saddle work. The tall bay would scarcely know how to keep his feet out of gopher-holes in such a chase as was now inaugurated.

"Be careful how you use your guns," Frances said, quietly, when Sam and the Mexican, with the dogs, started off to round a certain greasewood-covered mound and see if they could start some of the long-eared animals.

"Never fire across your pony's neck unless you

are positive that no other rider is ahead of you on either hand.   Better take your rabbit head on; then the danger of shooting into some of the rest of us will be eliminated."

Sue sniffed at this.   She had no gun, of course, but almost wished she had—and she said as much to one of her friends.   She'd show that range girl that she couldn't boss her!

"Why! that's good advice about using our guns," said this girl to whom Sue complained, surprised at the objection.

"Pooh! what does she know about it?   She puts herself forward too much," replied the girl from Boston.

It is probable that Sue would have talked about any other girl in the party who seemed to take the lead.   Sue was used to being the leader herself, and if she couldn't lead she didn't wish to follow. There are more than a few people in the world of Sue's temperament—and very unpleasant people they are.

But it was Frances who got the first jack.   The creature came leaping down the slope, having broken cover at the brink and quite unseen by the rest of the hunters.

This was business to Frances, instead of sport. If allowed to multiply the jack-rabbits were not only a pest to the farmers, but to everybody else.

Frances raised the light firearm she carried and popped Mr. Longears over " on the fly."

" Glory! that's a good one!" shouted Pratt, enthusiastically.

" A clean hit, Frances," said Mrs. Edwards. " You are a splendid shot, child."

Miss Boston sniffed!

The dogs did not bay. But in a minute or two a pair of the rabbits appeared over the rise, and then the two long-legged canines followed in their tracks.

" Wait till the jacks see us and dodge," called out Frances, in a low tone. " Then you can fire without getting the dogs in line."

Mrs. Edwards was a good shot. She got one of the rabbits. After several of the others snapped at the second one, and missed him, Frances brought him down just as he leaped toward a clump of sagebrush. Behind it he would have been lost to them.

" My goodness!" murmured Pratt. " What a shot you are, Frances!"

" She's quite got the best of us in shooting," complained one of the other girls. " She'll bag them all."

Frances laughed, and spurred Molly out of the group. " I'll put away my gun and use my rope instead," she remarked. " Perhaps I *have* a handicap over the rest of you with a rifle. Father taught me, and he is considered the best rifle shot in the Panhandle."

" My goodness, Frances," said Pratt again. " What isn't there that you don't do better than most of 'em? "

" Parlor tricks! " flashed back the girl of the ranges, half laughing, but half in earnest, too. " I know I should be just a silly with a lorgnette, or trying to tango."

" Well! " gasped the young fellow, " who isn't silly under those circumstances, I would like to know."

Mixing talk of lorgnettes and dancing with shooting jack-rabbits did not suit very well, for the next pair of the long-eared animals that the dogs started got away entirely.

They rode on down the edge of the hollow through which the stream flowed. The dogs beat the bushes and cottonwood clumps. Suddenly a small, graceful, spotted animal leaped from concealment and came up the slope of the long river-bank ahead of both the dogs and almost under the noses of some of the excited ponies.

" Oh! an antelope! " shrieked two or three of the young people, recognizing the graceful creature.

" Don't shoot it! " cried Mrs. Edwards. " I

am not sure that the law will let us touch antelopes at this season.

"You needn't fear, Mrs. Edwards," said the girl from Boston, laughing. "Nobody is likely to get near enough to shoot that creature. Wonderful! see how it leaps. Why! those funny dogs couldn't even catch it."

Frances had had no idea of touching the antelope. But suddenly she spurred Molly away at an angle from the bank, and called to the dogs to keep on the trail of the little deer.

"Ye-hoo! Go for it! On, boys!" she shouted, and already the rope was swinging about her head.

Pratt spurred after her, and by chance Sue Latrop's pony got excited and followed the two madly. Sue could not pull him in.

The antelope did not seem to be half trying, he bounded along so gracefully and easily. The long-limbed dogs were doing their very best. The ponies were coming down upon the quarry at an acute angle.

The antelope's beautiful, spidery legs flashed back and forth like piston-rods, or the spokes of a fast-rolling wheel. They could scarcely be seen clearly. In five minutes the antelope would have drawn far enough away from the chase to be safe —and he could have kept up his pace for half an hour.

Frances was near, however. Molly, coming on the jump, gave the girl of the ranges just the chance that she desired. She arose suddenly in her saddle, leaned forward, and let the loop fly.

Like a snake it writhed in the air, and then settled just before the leaping antelope. The creature put its forelegs and head fairly into the whirring circle!

The moment before—figuring with a nicety that made Pratt Sanderson gasp with wonder—Frances had pulled back on Molly's bit and jerked back her own arm that controlled the lasso.

Molly slid on her haunches, while the loop tightened and held the antelope in an unbreakable grip.

"Quick, Pratt!" cried the girl of the ranges, seeing the young man coming up. "Get down and use your knife. He'll kick free in a second."

As Pratt obeyed, leaping from his saddle before the grey pony really halted, Sue Latrop raced up on her mount and stopped. Frances was leaning back in her saddle, holding the rope as taut as possible. Pratt flung himself upon the struggling antelope.

And then rather a strange and unexpected thing happened. Pratt had the panting, quivering, frightened creature in his arms. A thrust of his hunting knife would have put it out of all pain.

Sue was as eager as one of the hounds which were now coming up with great leaps. Pratt glanced around a moment, saw the dogs coming, and suddenly loosened the noose and let the antelope go free.

"What are you doing?" shrieked the girl from Boston. "You've let it go!"

"Yes," said Pratt, quietly.

"But what for?" demanded Sue, quite angrily. "Why! you had it."

"Yes," said Pratt again, as the two girls drew near to him.

"You—you—why! what for?" repeated Sue, half-bewildered.

"I couldn't bear to kill it, or let the dogs tear it," said Pratt, slowly. The antelope was now far away and Frances had commanded the dogs to return.

"Why not?" asked Sue, grimly.

"Because the poor little thing was crying—actually!" gasped Pratt, very red in the face. "Great tears were running out of its beautiful eyes. I could have killed a helpless baby just as easily."

Frances coiled up her line and never said a word. But Sue flashed out:

"Oh, you gump! I've been in at the death of a fox a number of times and seen the brush cut off and the dogs worry the beast to death. That's

what they are for.   Well, you are a softy, Pratt
Sanderson."

"I guess I am," admitted the young bank clerk.
"I wasn't made for such work as this."

He turned away to catch his pony and did not
even look at Frances.   If he had, he would have
seen her eyes illuminated with a radiant admiration
that would almost have stunned him.

"If daddy had seen him do that," whispered
Frances to herself, "I'm sure he would have a better opinion of Pratt than he has.   I am certain
that nobody with so tender a heart could be really
bad."

But the incident separated the range girl from
the young man from Amarillo for the time being.
Silent Sam and Frances had some trouble in getting the dogs off the antelope trail.

When they started the next bunch of jack-
rabbits from the brush, Frances was with the foreman and the Mexican boy, and acted with them as
beaters.   The visitors had great fun bagging the
animals.

Frances, rather glad to escape from the crowd
for a time, spurred Molly down the far side of
the stream, having crossed it in a shallow place.
She was out of sight of the hunters, and soon out
of sound.   They had turned back and were going
up stream again.

The ranchman's daughter pulled in Molly at the brink of a little hollow beside the stream. There was a cleared space in the centre and—yes—there was a fireplace and ashes. Thick brush surrounded the camping place save on the side next to the stream.

"Wonder who could have been here? And recently, too. There's smoke rising from those embers."

This was Frances' unspoken thought. She let Molly step nearer. Trees overhung the place. She saw that it was as secret a spot as she had seen along the river side, and her thought flashed to Pete, the ex-orderly of the Bylittle Soldiers' Home.

Then she turned in her saddle suddenly and saw the very man standing near her, rifle in hand. His leering smile frightened her.

Although he said never a word, Frances' hand tightened on Molly's rein. The next moment she would have spurred the pinto up the hill; but a drawling voice within a yard of her spoke.

"How-do, Frances? 'Light, won't yer?" and there followed Ratty M'Gill's well-known laugh. "We didn't expect ye; but ye're welcome just the same."

Ratty's hand was on Molly's bridle-rein. Frances knew that she was a prisoner.

CHAPTER XXII

THE party of visitors to the Edwards ranch tired of jack-shooting and jack-running before noon. José Reposa had cached a huge hamper of lunch which the Bar-T cook had put up, and he softly suggested to Mrs. Edwards that the company be called together and luncheon made ready, with hot coffee for all.

" But where's Pratt? " cried somebody.

" And Miss Rugley? " asked another.

" Oh, I guess you'll find them together somewhere," snapped Sue Latrop.

She had felt neglected by her " hero " for the last hour, and was in the sulks, accordingly.

Pratt, however, came in alone. He had bagged several jacks. Altogether Silent Sam and the Mexican had destroyed more than a score of the pests, and the dogs had torn to pieces two or three beside. The canines were satiated with the meat, and were glad to lie down, panting, and watch the preparations for luncheon.

"I have not seen Miss Frances since she caught the antelope," Pratt declared.

Sue began to laugh—but it wasn't a nice laugh at all. "Guess she got mad and went home. You, letting that animal go the way you did! I never heard of such a foolish thing!"

Pratt said nothing. He sat down on the other side of the fire from the girl from Boston. He took it for granted that Frances *had* gone home.

For, remembering as he did, that Frances was a range girl, and had lived out-of-doors and undoubtedly among rough men, a good part of her life, the young fellow thought that, very probably, Frances had been utterly disgusted with him when he showed so much tenderness for the innocent little antelope.

Since that moment of weakness he had been telling himself:

"She thinks me a softy. I am. What kind of a hunter did I show myself to be? Pooh! she must be disgusted with my weakness."

Nevertheless, he would have done the same thing over again. It was his nature not to wish to see dumb creatures in pain, or to inflict pain on them himself.

Killing the jack-rabbits was a necessity as well as a sport. Even chasing a poor, unfortunate little fox, as Sue had done in the East, might be made to seem a commendable act, for the foxes, when numerous, are a nuisance around the poultry runs.

But by no possible reasoning could Pratt have ever excused his killing of the pretty, innocent antelope. They did not need it for food, and it was one of the most harmless creatures in the world.

To tell the truth, Pratt was glad Frances was not present at the luncheon. He cared a good deal less about Sue's saucy tongue than he did for the range girl's opinion of him.

During these weeks that he had known Frances Rugley, he had come to see that hers was a most vigorous and interesting character. Pratt was a thoughtful young man. There was nothing foolish about his interest in Frances, but he *did* crave her friendship and liking.

Some of the other men rallied him on his sudden silence, and this gave Sue Latrop an opportunity to say more sarcastic things.

" He misses that ' cattle queen,' " she giggled, but was careful that Mrs. Edwards did not hear what she said. " Too bad; poor little boy! Why didn't you ride after her, Pratt? "

" I might, had I known when she went home," replied Pratt, cheerfully.

" I beg the Señor's pardon," whispered José,

who was gathering up the plates.   "The *señorita*
did not go home."

Pratt looked at the boy, sharply.   "Sure?" he
asked.

"Quite so—*si, señor.*"

"Where did she go?"

"*Quien sabe?*" retorted José Reposa, with a
shrug of his shoulders.   "She crossed the river
yonder and rode east."

So did the party from the Edwards ranch a
little later.   Silent Sam Harding had already ridden back to the Bar-T.   José gathered up the
hamper and its contents and started home on mule-
back.

Pratt had curiosity enough, when the party went
over the river, to look for the prints of Molly's
hoofs.

There they were in the soft earth on the far
edge of the stream.   Frances had ridden down
stream at a sharp pace.   Where had she gone?

"It was odd for her to leave us in that way,"
thought Pratt, turning the matter over in his mind,
"and not to return.   In a way she was our hostess.
I did not think Frances would fail in any matter of
courtesy.   How could she with Captain Dan Rugley for a father?"

The old ranchman was the soul of hospitality.
That Frances should seem to ignore her duty as a

hostess stung Pratt keenly.   He heard Sue Latrop speaking about it.

"Went off mad.   What else could you expect of a cowgirl?" said the girl from Boston, in her very nastiest tone.

The fact that Sue seemed so sure Frances was derelict in her duty made Pratt more confident that something untoward had occurred to the girl of the ranges to keep her from returning promptly to the party.

Of course, the young man suspected nothing of the actual situation in which Frances at that very moment found herself.   Pratt dreamed of a broken cinch, or a misstep that might have lamed Molly.

Instead, Frances Rugley was sitting with her back against a stump at the edge of the clearing where she had come so suddenly upon the camp-fire, with her ungloved hands lying in her lap so that Ratty's bright eyes could watch them continually.

Pete had taken away her gun.   Molly was hobbled with the men's horses on the other side of the hollow.   The two plotters had rekindled the fire and were whispering together about her.

Had Pete had his way he would have tied Frances' hands and feet.   But the ex-cowpuncher of the Bar-T ranch would not listen to that.

Although Pete was the leading spirit, Ratty M'Gill turned ugly when his mate attempted to touch the girl; so they had left her unbound. But not unwatched—no, indeed! Ratty's beadlike eyes never left her.

Not much of their conversation reached the ears of Frances, although she kept very still and tried to hear. She could read Ratty's lips a little, for he had no mustache; but the bearded Pete's lips were hidden.

" I've got to have a good piece of it myself, if I'm going to take a chance like that!" was one declaration of the ex-cowpuncher's that she heard clearly.

Again Ratty said: " They'll not only suspect me, they'll *know*. Won't the girl tell them? I tell you I want to see my getaway before I make a stir in the matter—you can bet on that! "

Finally, Frances saw the ex-orderly of the Bylittle Soldiers' Home produce a pad of paper, an envelope, and pencil. He was plainly a ready writer, for he went to work with the pencil at once, while Ratty rolled a fresh cigarette and still watched their captive.

Pete finished his letter, sealed it in the envelope, and addressed it in a bold hand.

" That'll just about fix the business, I reckon," said Pete, scowling across at Frances. " That

gal's mighty smart—with her trunk full of junk
and all—— "

Ratty burst into irrepressible laughter.   "You
sure got Pete's goat when you played him that
trick, Frances.   He fair killed himself puntin' that
trunk up the river and hiding it, and then taking
the punt back and letting it drift so as to put Peckham's crew off the scent.

"And when he busted it open—— " Ratty burst
into laughter again, and held his sides.   Pete
looked surly.

"We'll make the old man pay for her cuttin'
up them didoes," growled the bewhiskered rascal.
"And my horse and wagon, too.   I b'lieve she
and that man with her set the fire that burned up
my outfit."

Frances herewith took part in the conversation.

"Who set the grass-fire, in the first place?" she
demanded.   "I believe you did that, Ratty M'Gill.
You were just reckless enough that day."

"Aw, shucks!" said the young man, sheepishly.

"But you haven't the same excuse to-day for
being reckless," the girl said, earnestly.   "You
have not been drinking.   What do you suppose
Sam and the boys will do to you for treating me in
this manner?"

"Now, that will do!" said Pete, hoarsely.
"You hold your tongue, young woman!"

But Ratty only laughed. He accepted the letter, took off his sombrero, tucked it under the sweatband, and put on the hat again. Then he started lazily for the pony that he rode.

" Now mind you! " he called back over his shoulder to Pete, " I'm not going to risk my scalp going to the ranch-house with this yere billy-do— not much ! "

" Why not? " asked Pete, angrily. " We got to move quick."

" We'll move quick later; we'll go sure and steady now," chuckled the cowboy. "I'll send it in by one of the Mexicans. Say it was give to me by a stranger on the trail. I ain't welcome at the Bar-T, and I know it."

He leaped into his saddle and spurred his horse away, quickly getting out of sight. Frances knew that the letter he carried, and which Pete had written, was to her father.

CHAPTER XXIII

A GAME OF PUSS IN THE CORNER

THE reckless cowpuncher, Ratty M'Gill, riding up the bank of the narrow stream through the cottonwoods, and singing a careless song at the top of his voice, was what gave Pratt Sanderson the final suggestion that there was something down stream that he ought to look into.

Frances had gone that way; Ratty was riding back. Had they met, or passed, on the river bank?

Of the cavalcade cutting across the range for Mr. Edwards' place, Pratt was the only member that noticed the discharged cowpuncher. And he waited until the latter was well out of sight and hearing before he turned his grey pony's head back toward the river.

" Where are you going, Pratt? " demanded one of his friends.

" I've forgotten something," the young man from Amarillo replied.

" Oh, dear me! " cried Sue Latrop. " He's forgotten his cute, little cattle queen. Give her my love, Pratt."

The young fellow did not reply. If the girl from Boston had really been of sufficient importance, Pratt would have hated her. Sue had made herself so unpleasant that she could never recover her place in his estimation—that was sure!

He set spurs to his pony and raced away before any other remarks could be made in his hearing. He rode directly back to the ford they had crossed; but reaching it, he turned sharply down stream, in the direction from which Ratty M'Gill had come.

Here and there in the soft earth he saw the marks of Molly's hoofs. But when these marks were no longer visible on the harder ground, Pratt kept on.

He soon pulled the grey down to a walk. They made little noise, he and the pony. Two miles he rode, and then suddenly the grey pony pointed his ears forward.

Pratt reached quickly and seized the grey's nostrils between thumb and finger. In the distance a pony whinnied. Was it Molly?

" You just keep still, you little nuisance! " whispered Pratt to his mount. " Don't want you whinnying to any strange horse."

He got out of the saddle and led his pony for some rods. The brush was thick and there was no bridle-path. He feared to go farther without knowing what and who was ahead, and he tied the grey—taking pattern by Frances and tying his head up-wind.

The young fellow hesitated about taking the shotgun he had used in the jack-rabbit hunt. There was a sheath fastened to his saddle for the weapon, and he finally left it therein.

Pratt really thought that nothing of a serious nature had happened to his girl friend. Seeing Ratty M'Gill had reminded him that the cow-puncher had once troubled Frances, and Pratt had ridden down this way to offer his escort to the old ranchman's daughter.

He had no thought of the man who had held them up at the lower ford, toward Peckham's, the evening of the prairie fire; nor did he connect the cowpuncher and that ruffian in his mind.

"If I take that gun, the muzzle will make a noise in the bushes, or the hammer will catch on something," thought Pratt.

So he left the shotgun behind and went on un-armed toward the place where Frances was even then sitting under the keen eye of Pete.

"You keep where ye are, Miss," growled that worthy when Ratty rode away. "I will sure tie ye if ye make an attempt to get away. You have fell right into my han's, and I vow you'll make me some money. Your father's got a plenty—— "

"You mean to make him ransom me?" asked Frances, quietly.

"That's the ticket," said Pete, nodding, and searching his ragged clothing for a pipe, which he finally drew out and filled. "He's got money. I've spent what I brought up yere to the Panhandle with me. And I b'lieve you made me lose my wagon and that other horse."

Frances made no rejoinder to this last, but she said:

"Father may be willing to pay something for my release. But you and Ratty will suffer in the end."

"We'll risk that," said the man, puffing at his pipe, and nodding thoughtfully.

"You'd better let me go now," said the girl, with no display of fear. "And you'd better give up any further attempt to get at the old chest that Mr. Lonergan talked about."

"Hey!" exclaimed the man, startled. "What d'ye know about Lonergan?"

"He will be at the ranch in a few days, and if there is any more treasure than you found in that old trunk you stole from me, he will get his share and there will no longer be any treasure chest. Make up your mind to that."

"You know who I am and what I come up yere for?" demanded Pete, eying her malevolently.

"Yes. I know you are the man who tried to steal in over the roof of our house, too. If you make my father any angrier with you than he is now, he will prosecute you all the more sharply when you are arrested."

"You shut up!" growled Pete. "I ain't going to be arrested."

"Both you and Ratty will be punished in the end," said Frances, calmly. "Men like you always are."

"Lots you know about it, Sissy. And don't you be too sassy, understand? I could squeeze yer breath out!"

He stretched forth a clawlike hand as he spoke, and pinched the thumb and finger wickedly to-gether. That expression and gesture was the first thing that really frightened the girl—it was so wicked!

She shuddered and fell back against the tree trunk. Never in her life before had Frances Rugley felt so nearly hysterical. The realization that she was in this man's power, and that he had reason to hate her, shook her usually steady nerves.

After all, Ratty M'Gill was little more than a reckless boy; but this older man was vile and bad. As he squatted over the fire, puffing at his pipe, with his head craned forward, he looked like nothing so much as a bald-headed buzzard, such as she had seen roosting on dead trees or old barn-roofs, outside of Amarillo.

Pete finally knocked the ashes out of his pipe on his boot heel and then arose. Frances could scarcely contain herself and suppress a scream when he moved. She watched him with fearful gaze—and perhaps the fellow knew it.

It may have been his intention to work upon her fears in just this way. Brave as the range girl was, her helplessness was not to be ignored. She knew that she was at his mercy.

When he shot a sideways glance at her as he stretched his powerful arms and stamped his feet and yawned, he must have seen the color come and go faintly in her cheeks.

Rough as were the men Frances had been brought up with—for from babyhood she had been with her father in cow-camp and bunk-house and corral—she had always been accorded a perfectly chivalrous treatment which is natural to men of the open.

Where there are few women, and those utterly dependent for safety upon the manliness of the men, the latter will always rise to the very highest instincts of the race.

Frances had been utterly fearless while riding herd, or camping with the cowboys, or even when alone on the range. If she met strange men she expected and received from them the courtesy for which the Western man is noted.

But this leering fellow was different from any person with whom Frances had ever come in contact before.   Each moment she became more fearful of him.

And he realized her attitude of fear and worked upon her emotions until she was almost ready to burst out into hysterical screams.

Indeed, she might have done this very thing the next time Pete came near her had not suddenly a voice spoken her name.

" Frances! what is the matter with you? "

" Oh! " she gasped.   " Pratt! "

The young man stepped out of the bushes, not seeing Pete at all.   He had been watching the girl only, and had not understood what made her look so strange.

" You haven't been thrown, Frances, have you? " asked Pratt, solicitously.   " Are you hurt? "

Then the girl's frightened gaze, or some rustle of Pete's movement, made Pratt Sanderson turn.   Pete had reached for his rifle and secured it.   And by so doing he completely mastered the situation.

" Put your hands over your head, young feller! " he growled, swinging the muzzle of the heavy gun toward Pratt. "And keep 'em there till I've seen what you carry in your pockets."

He strode toward the surprised Pratt, who obeyed the order with becoming promptness.

"Don't you make no move, neither, Miss," growled the man, darting a glance in Frances' direction.

"Why—why—— What do you mean?" demanded Pratt, recovering his breath at last. "Do you dare hold this young lady a prisoner?"

"Yep. That's what I dare," sneered Pete. "And it looks like I'd got you, too. What d'ye think you're going to do about it?"

"Isn't this the fellow who robbed us at the river that time, Frances?" cried Pratt.

The girl nodded. Just then she could not speak.

"And that fellow Ratty was with him this time?"

Again the girl nodded.

"Then they shall both be arrested and punished," declared Pratt. "I never heard of such effrontery. Do you know who this young lady is, man?" he demanded of Pete.

"Jest as well as you do. And her pa's going to put up big for to see her again—unharmed," snarled the man.

"What do you mean?" gasped Pratt, his face

blazing and his fists clenched.   " You dare harm her—— "

Pete was slapping him about the pockets to make sure he carried no weapon.   Now he struck Pratt a heavy blow across the mouth, cutting his lips and making his ears ring.

" Shut up, you young jackanapes ! " commanded the man.   " I'll hurt her and you, too, if I like."

" And Captain Dan Rugley won't rest till he sees you well punished if you harm her," mumbled Pratt.

Pete struck at him again.   Pratt dodged back. 'And at that moment Frances disappeared !

The man had only had his eyes off her for half a minute.   He gasped, his jaw dropped, and his bloodshot eyes roved all about, trying to discover Frances' whereabouts.

He had not realized that, despite her fear, the girl of the ranges had had her limbs drawn up and her muscles taut ready for a spring.

His attention given for the moment to Pratt Sanderson, Frances had risen and dodged behind the bole of the tree against which she was leaning, a carefully watched prisoner.

She would never have escaped so easily had it been Ratty in charge; for his mental processes were quicker than those of Pete.

Flitting from tree to tree, keeping one or more

of the big trunks between her and Pete's roving
eyes while still he was speechless, she was traveling
farther and farther from the camp.

She might have set forth running almost at
once, and so escaped. But she could not leave
Pratt to the heavy hand of Pete. Nor could she
abandon Molly.

Frances, therefore, began encircling the opening
where the fire burned; but she kept well out of
Pete's sight.

She heard him utter a bellow which would have
done credit to a mad steer. That came when he
saw Pratt was about to escape, too.

The young fellow was creeping away, stooping
and on tiptoe. Pete uttered a frightful impreca-
tion and sprang after him with his rifle clubbed and
raised above his head.

"Stand where you are!" he commanded, "or
I'll bat your foolish head in!"

And he looked enraged enough to do it. Pratt
dared not move farther; he crouched in terror,
expecting the blow.

He had bravely assailed Pete with his tongue
when Frances seemed in danger; but the girl had
escaped now and Pratt hoped she was each minute
putting rods between this place and herself.

Pete suddenly dropped his rifle and sprang at
the young man. Pratt's throat was in the vicelike

grip of Pete on the instant. Both his wrists were seized by the man's other hand.

Such feeble struggles as Pratt made were abortive. His breath was shut off and he felt his senses leaving him.

But as his eyes rolled up there was a crash in the brush and a pony dashed into the open. It was Molly and her mistress was astride her.

Frances had lost her hat; her hair had become loosened and was tossed about her pale face. But her eyes glowed with the light of determination and she spurred the pony directly at the two struggling figures in the middle of the hollow.

" I'm coming, Pratt! " she cried. " Hold on ! "

CHAPTER XXIV

A GOOD DEAL OF EXCITEMENT

PETE twisted himself around to look over his shoulder, but still kept his clutch on the breathless young man. However, Pratt feebly dragged his wrists out of the man's grasp.

Frances was riding the pinto directly at them. Under her skillful guidance the pony's off shoulder must collide with Pete, unless the man dropped Pratt entirely and sprang aside.

The man did this, uttering a yell of anger. Pratt staggered the other way and Frances brought Molly to a standstill directly between the two.

"You let him alone!" the girl commanded, gazing indignantly at the rascally man. "Oh! you shall be paid in full for all you have done this day. When Captain Rugley hears of this.

"Quick, Pratt!" she shrieked. "That rifle!"

Pete was bent over reaching for the weapon. Frances jerked Molly around, but she could not drive the pony against the man in time to topple him over before his wicked fingers closed on the barrel of the gun.

It was Pratt who made the attack in this emergency. He had played on the Amarillo High football eleven and he knew how to " tackle."

Before Pete could rise up with the recovered weapon in his grasp Pratt had him around the legs. The man staggered forward, trying to kick away the young fellow; but Pratt clung to him, and his antagonist finally fell upon his knees.

Quick as a flash Pratt sprang astride his bowed back. He kicked Pete's braced arms out from under him and the man fell forward, screaming and threatening the most awful punishment for his young antagonist.

Frances could not get into the mêlée with Molly. The two rolled over and over on the ground and suddenly Pete gave vent to a shriek of pain. He had rolled on his back into the fire!

" Quick, Pratt! " begged Frances. " Get away from him! He will do you some dreadful harm! "

She believed Pete would, too. As Pratt leaped aside, the man bounded up from the bed of hot coals, his shirt afire, and he unable to reach it with his beating hands!

Pratt ran to Frances' side. She pulled Molly's head around and the pony trotted across the clearing, with Pratt staggering along at the stirrup and striving to get his breath.

As they passed the spot where the battle had

begun, Pratt stooped and secured the rifle. Pete, in rage awful to see, was tearing the smouldering shirt from his back. Then Pete dashed after the escaping pair.

The rifle encumbered the young man; but if he dropped it he knew the man would hold them at his mercy. So, swinging the weapon up by its barrel, he smashed the stock against a tree trunk.

Again and again he repeated the blow, until the tough wood splintered and the mechanism of the hammer and trigger was bent and twisted. Pete almost caught him. Pratt dashed the remains of the rifle in his face and ran on after Frances.

" I'll catch you yet! " yelled Pete. " And when I do—— "

The threat was left incomplete; but the man ran for his own horse.

If Frances had only thought to drive Molly that way and slip the hobbles of Pete's nag, much of what afterward occurred in this hollow by the river bank would never have taken place. She and Pratt would have been immediately free.

It was hours afterward—indeed, almost sunset —that old Captain Rugley, sitting on the broad veranda of the Bar-T ranch-house and expecting Frances to appear at any moment, raised his eyes to see, instead, Victorino Reposa slouching up the steps.

"Hello, Vic!" said the Captain. "What do you want?"

"Letter, *Capitan*," said the Mexican, impassively, removing his big hat and drawing a soiled envelope from within.

"Seen anything of Miss Frances?" asked the ranchman, reaching lazily for the missive.

"No, *Capitan*," responded the boy, and turned away.

The superscription on the envelope puzzled Captain Dan Rugley. "Here, Vic!" he cried after the departing youth. "Where'd you get this? 'Tisn't a mailed letter."

"It was give to me on the trail, *Capitan*," said Victorino, softly. "As I came back from the horse pasture."

"Who gave it to you?" demanded the ranchman, beginning to slit the flap of the envelope.

"I am not informed," said Victorino, still with lowered gaze. "The Señor who presented it declare' it was give to heem by a strange hand at Jackleg. He say he was ride this way——"

The Captain was not listening. Victorino saw that this was a fact and he allowed his words to trail off into nothing, while he, himself, began again to slip away.

The old ranchman was staring at the unfolded sheet with fixed attention. His brows came together in a portentous frown; and perhaps for the first time in many years his bronzed countenance was washed over by the sickly pallor of fear.

Victorino, stepping softly, had reached the compound gate. Suddenly the forelegs of the ranchman's chair hit the floor of the veranda, and he roared at the Mexican in a voice that made the latter jump and drop the brown paper cigarette he had just deftly rolled.

"You boy! Come back here!" called Captain Rugley. "I want to know what this means."

"Me, *Capitan?*" asked Victorino, softly, and hesitated at the gate. With his employer in this temper he was half-inclined to run in the opposite direction.

"Come here!" commanded the ranchman again. "Who gave you this?" rapping the open letter with a hairy forefinger.

"I do not know, *Capitan*. A strange man—*si.*"

"Never saw him before?"

"No, *Capitan*. He was ver' strange to me," whined Victorino, too frightened to tell the truth.

"What did he look like?" shot back the Captain, holding himself in splendid control now. Only his eyes glittered and his lips under the big mustache tightened perceptibly.

"He was beeg man, *Capitan;* rode bay pony;

much wheeskers on face," declared Victorino, glibly.

The Captain was silent for half a minute. Then he snapped: " Run find Silent Sam and tell him I want him *pronto. Sabe?* Tell Joe to saddle Cherry, and Sam's horse, and you get a saddle on your own, Vic. I'll want you and about half a dozen of the boys who are hanging around the bunk-house. Tell 'em it's important and tell them —yes!—tell them to come armed. In fifteen minutes. Understand? "

" *Si, Capitan,*" whispered Victorino, glad to get out from under the ranchman's eye for the time being.

He was the oldest of the Mexican boys employed at the Bar-T, and he had been very friendly with Ratty M'Gill while that reckless individual had belonged to the outfit.

It was Victorino who had let Ratty drive the buckboard to the railroad station one particular day when the cowpuncher wished to meet his friend, Pete, at Cottonwood Bottom.

Now, unthinking and unknowing, he had been drawn by Ratty into a serious trouble. Victorino did not know what it was; but he trembled. He had never seen *" El Capitan "* look so fierce and strange before.

CHAPTER XXV

A PLOT THAT FAILED

CAPTAIN DAN RUGLEY seemed to forget his rheumatism. Excitement is often a strong mental corrective; and with his mind upon the dearest possession of his old age, the ranchman forgot all bodily ills.

Victorino was scarcely out of the compound when the Captain had summoned Ming from the dining-room and San Soo from his pots and pans.

"Put off dinner. Maybe we won't have any dinner to-night, San Soo," said the owner of the Bar-T "We're in trouble. You and Ming shut the doors when I go out and bar them. Stand watch. Don't let a soul in unless I come back or Miss Frances appears. Understand, boys?"

"Can do," declared the bigger Chinaman, with impassive face.

"Me understland Clapen velly well," said Ming, who wished always to show that he "spoke Melican."

"All right," returned Captain Rugley. "Help me with this coat, San. Ming! Bring me my belt and gun. Yes, that's it. It's loaded. Plenty of cartridges in that box? So. Now I'm off," concluded the Captain, and went to the door again to meet Silent Sam Harding, the foreman.

"Read this," jerked out the ranchman, and thrust the crumpled letter into Sam Harding's hand.

Without a word the foreman spread open the paper and studied it. In perfectly plain handwriting he read the following astonishing epistle:

"Captain Dan Rugley,
    "Bar-T Ranch.
    "We've got your girl. She will be held prisoner exactly twenty-four hours from time you receive this. Then, if you have not made arrangements to pay our agent $5,000 (five thousand dolls.), something will happen to your girl. We are willing to put our necks in a noose for the five thousand. Come across, and come across quick. No check. Cash does it. You can get cash at branch bank in Jackleg. We will know when you get cash and then you'll be told who to hand money to and how to find your girl. Remember, we mean business. You try to trail us, or rescue your daughter without paying five thousand and we'll get square with you by fixing the girl. That's all at present."

This threatening missive was unsigned.   Silent
Sam read it twice.   Then he handed it back to the
Captain.

" Does it look like a joke to you—a poor sort
of a joke? " whispered the ranchman.

" I wouldn't say so," muttered Sam.

" I'm going after them," said Captain Rugley,
with determination.

" How? "

" Somebody handed Vic this on the trail.   He'll
show us where.   We'll try to pick up the man's
traces.   Of course it was one of the scoundrels
handed the letter to Vic."

" Who do ye think they are? " asked Sam,
slowly.

" I don't know," said the worried ranchman.
" But whoever they are they shall suffer if they
harm a hair of her head! "

" That's what," said Sam, quietly.   " But ain't
you an idee who they be? "

" That fellow who took the old trunk away
from Frances? "

" Might be.   And he must have partners."

" So I've said right along," declared the ranchman, vigorously.   " Where did you leave Frances,
Sam? "

" After the jack hunt?   Right thar with Miz'
Edwards and her crowd."

" Was young Pratt Sanderson with them? "

" Sure."

" That's it! " growled Captain Dan Rugley, smiting one palm with his other fist. " She'd ride off with him.   Thinks him all right—— "

" Ye don't mean to say ye think he's in this mean mess? "

" I don't know.   He's turned up whenever we've had trouble lately.   If it wasn't so far to Bill Edwards' I'd ride that way and find out if the fellow is there, or what they know about him."

Silent Sam earned his nickname, if ever, during the next hour.   He did not say ten words; but his efficient management got a posse of the most trustworthy men together, and they rode away from the ranch-house.

There was no use advising the Captain not to accompany the party.   Nobody dared thwart him after a glance into his grim face.

The hard-bitted Cherry which he always rode was held down to the pace of the other horses with an iron hand.   The Captain rode as securely in his saddle as he had before rheumatism seized upon his limbs.

How long this false strength, inspired by his fear and indignation, would remain with him the others did not know.   Sam and his mates watched " the Old Cap " with wonder.

Victorino's gaze was fixed upon the doughty ranchman's back with many different emotions in his trouble-torn mind. He was wondering what would happen to him if Captain Rugley ever learned that he had told a falsehood about that note.

He was so scared that he dared not lead the party to a false trail. He told them just where he had met Ratty M'Gill; but he stuck to his imaginary description of the person who had entrusted the letter to him.

" Going, west, you say? " said Captain Rugley. " It might be to lead us off the trail. And then again, he might be going right back to whatever place they have Frances hidden.

" I fear we'll have a hard time following a trail to-night, anyway. But Sam says he left the folks after the jack hunt over there by Cottonwood Bottom. I think we'd better search the length of that stream first."

Sam spoke up suddenly: " Frances asked me if there were any close thickets where a man might hide out, along those banks."

" She did? "

" Yes. It just come to me," said the foreman. " When we were beating up those jacks."

" Enough said! " ejaculated the ranchman. " Come on, boys! "

Through the dusk they rode straight away toward the ford.   And although the old Captain could hardly hope it, every moment the horse was bearing him nearer and nearer to his lost daughter.

Dusk had long since fallen; but there was a faint moon and a multitude of stars.   On the open plain the shadows of the horses and riders moved in grotesque procession.   In the hollow far down the stream, where Pete had made his camp, the shadows were deep and oppressive.

The fellow kept alive but a spark of fire.   Now and then he threw on a stick for replenishing. Outside the feeble light cast by the flickering flames, one could scarcely see at all.

But there were two faintly outlined forms near the fire beside that of the burly Pete.   Occasionally a groan issued from the lips of Pratt Sanderson, for he lay senseless, a great bruise upon his head, his wrists and ankles tied with painful security.

The other form was that of Frances herself. She did not speak nor moan, although she was quite wideawake.   She, too, was tied up in such a way that she could not possibly free herself.

And she was frightened—desperately frightened!

She had reason to be.   The ex-orderly from the Bylittle Soldiers' Home had proved himself to be a perfect madman when he found that the girl and Pratt were really escaping.

Evidently he had seized upon the desperate attempt to hold Frances for ransom as a last resort. She had played into his hands by riding down into this hollow.

Pratt Sanderson's interference had enraged the fellow to the limit.   And when the young man had momentarily gotten the best of him, Pete was fairly insane for the time being.

With his rifle broken the man was unable to shoot, for Frances' revolver which he had obtained at the beginning of the scuffle was empty.   The small gun she had used shooting jacks had been sent back with Sam to the ranch.

The girl was urging Molly through the brush and Pratt was tearing after her, their direction bringing them nearer and nearer to the young man's grey pony, when suddenly Frances heard Pratt scream.

She glanced back, pulling in the excited pinto with a strong hand.   Her friend was pitching forward to the ground.   He had been struck by her pistol, which Pete had flung with all his might.

The next moment with an exultant cry the man sprang from his horse upon the prostrate Pratt.

"Get off him!   Go away!" cried Frances, pulling Molly around.

But the brush was too thick, and the pinto got tangled up in it. Fearful for Pratt's safety, and never thinking of her own, the girl sprang from the saddle and ran back.

This was what Pete was expecting. Pratt was safe enough—senseless and moaning on the ground.

When the girl came near Pete leaped up, seized her by the wrists, jerked her toward him, and held her firmly with one hand while he produced a soiled bandanna, with which he quickly knotted her wrists together.

No matter how hard she fought, he was so much more powerful than she that the ranchman's daughter could not break his hold.   In five minutes she was tied and thrown to the ground, quite as helpless as Pratt himself.

Pete left her lying where she fell and picked up Pratt first.   Him the fellow carried back to the campfire and tied both hand and foot before he returned for Frances.

All the time the man uttered the most fearful imprecations, and showed so much callousness toward the injured young man that the girl begged him, with tears, to do something to ease Pratt.

" Let him lie there and grunt," growled Pete. " Didn't he chuck me into that fire? My back's all blistered."

He pulled on a coat, for his clothes had been quite torn away above his waist at the back when he was putting out the fire.

Frances suffered keenly herself, for the man had tied her wrists and ankles so tightly that the cords cut into the flesh whenever she tried to move them. Beside, she lay in a most uncomfortable position.

But to hear Pratt groan was terrible. The blow on the head had seriously hurt him—of that there could be no doubt. When she called to him he did not answer, and finally Pete commanded her to keep silence.

"Ye want to make a fuss so as to draw somebody down here—I kin see what you are up to."

Frances had a wholesome fear of him by this time. She had seen Pete at his worst—and had felt his heavy hand, too. She was bruised and suffering pain herself. But Pratt's case was much worse than her own just then and her whole heart went out to the young man from Amarillo.

Pete sat over his little fire and smoked. He was evidently expecting Ratty M'Gill to return; but for some reason Ratty was delayed.

Doubtless the two plotters had proposed to themselves that Captain Rugley would be too ill to take the lead in any chase after the kidnappers. Perhaps Pete even hoped that the old ranchman would agree immediately to the terms of ransom set forth in the note Ratty had taken to the Bar-T.

The ex-cowpuncher was to linger around and see what would be done about the message to the Captain; then come here and report to Pete. And as the hours dragged by, and it drew near midnight, with no appearance of the messenger, the chief plotter grew more anxious.

He huddled over the fire, almost enclosing it with his arms and legs for warmth. Frances, lying beyond, and out of the puny radiance of its warmth, felt the chill of the night air keenly. Pete did not even offer her a blanket.

But her attention was engaged by thoughts of Pratt Sanderson's sufferings. The young man groaned faintly from time to time, but he gave no other sign of life.

As Frances lay shivering on the ground her keen senses suddenly apprehended a new sound. She raised her head a little and the sound was absent. She dropped back upon the earth again and it returned—a throbbing sound, distant, faint but insistent.

What could it be? Frances was first startled, then puzzled by it. Each time that she raised her head the noise drifted away; then it returned when her ear was against the ground.

" It's a horse—it's several horses," she finally whispered to herself. " Can it be——? "

She sat up suddenly.   Pete immediately commanded her to lie down.

" I'm cramped," said the girl, speaking clearly. " Can't you change these cords?   I won't try to run away."

" I'd hurt you if you did," growled the fellow. "And I ain't going to change them cords."

" Oh, do! " cried Frances, more loudly.

" Shut up and lay down there! " ordered Pete, raising his own voice.

" No, I will not! " retorted the girl, deliberately tempting Pete into one of his rages.   If he became angry and yelled at her all the better!

" Do what I tell ye! " exclaimed the man. " Ain't ye l'arned that I mean what I say yet? "

" I must move my limbs.   They're cramped and co-o-old! " wailed Frances, and she put a deal of energy into her cry.

Pete began to get stiffly to his feet.   " Do like I tell ye, and lie down—or I'll knock ye down! " he threatened.

At that the girl risked uttering a cry and shrank back with a semblance of fear.   Aye, there was more than a semblance of fear in the attitude, for she believed he would strike her.   She had shrieked, however, at the top of her voice.

" Shut your mouth, ye crazy thing! " exclaimed the man, and he leaped toward her.

Frances threw herself back upon the ground. She heard the clatter of hoofbeats approaching. They could be mistaken for no other sound.

"Daddy! Daddy! Help! Help!"

Her voice was piercing. The cry for her father was involuntary, for she believed him too ill to leave the ranch-house.

But the answering shout that came down the wind was unmistakable.

"Daddy! Daddy!" Frances cried again, eagerly, loudly.

Pete was about to strike her; but he darted back and stood erect. The horses were plunging madly down the hillside through the brush. The party of rescue was already upon the camp.

The scoundrelly Pete leaped away to reach his own horse. He must have found the creature quickly in the darkness; for before the men from the Bar-T pulled in their horses before the smouldering campfire, Frances heard the rush of Pete's old pony as it dashed away down the stream.

"Daddy!" cried Frances for a third time. "We're here—Pratt and I. Look out for Pratt; he's hurt. I'm all right."

"Somebody throw some brush on that fire!" commanded the old ranchman. "Let's see what's been doing here."

"Sam, take a couple of the boys and go after

that fellow. You can follow that horse by sound."

He climbed stiffly out of his own saddle, and when the firelight flashed up revealing the little glade to better purpose, it was Captain Dan Rugley who lifted Frances to her feet and cut her bonds.

CHAPTER XXVI

FRANCES IN SOFTER MOOD

IT was the next day but one and the *hacienda* and compound lay bathed in the hot sun of noonday. Captain Dan Rugley was leaning back in his usual hard chair and in his usual attitude on the veranda, fairly soaking up the rays of the orb of day.

"Beats all the medicine for rheumatism in the doctor's shop! " he was wont to declare.

Since his night ride to rescue his daughter he had become more like his old self than he had been for weeks. The excitement seemed to have chased away the last twinges of pain for the time being, and he was without fever.

Now he was watching a swift pony-rider coming his way along the trail and listening to the patter of light footsteps coming down the broad stairway behind him.

" Here comes Sam, Frances," the ranchman said, in a low voice. " I reckon he'll have some news."

The girl came to the door. She had discarded

her riding habit and was dressed in a soft, clinging house gown, cut low at the throat and giving her arms freedom to the elbow. She wore pretty stockings and pretty slippers on her feet. Instead of a quirt she carried a fan in her hand and there was a handkerchief tucked into her belt.

The chrysalis of the cowgirl had burst and this butterfly had emerged. Of late it was not often that Frances had " dolled up," as the old Captain called it. Now he said, enthusiastically:

" My! you do look sweet! What's all the dolling up for? Me? The Chinks? Or maybe that boy upstairs, eh? "

" For myself," said Frances, quietly. " Pratt is too sick to notice much what I wear, I guess. But I find that I have been paying too little attention to dress."

" Huh! " snorted the old ranchman.

" It is a woman's duty to make herself as beautiful and attractive as possible," said Frances, with a bright smile. "You know, I read that in a woman's paper."

" You surely did! " agreed the ranchman, and then turned to meet Silent Sam as that individual drew up to the step.

" What's the good word, Sam? " inquired the Captain.

" Got that Ratty. He's in the jail at Jackleg.

Like you said, I never told nobody but the sheriff what 'twas for you wanted him."

" That's right," said the Captain, gravely. " If the boys understood he was mixed up with this kidnapping business, I don't know what they would do."

" Right, Captain," said the foreman. " So the sheriff took him for being all lit up. Ratty won't sleep it off before to-morrow."

" And if they could catch that Pete What's-his-name by then—— "

" Ain't found hide nor hair of him," answered Silent Sam.

" Where do you reckon he went to, Sam ? "

" He didn't go with his horse, Captain. He fooled us."

" What? "

" That's so. Horse was found yisterday evenin' down beyand Peckham's—scurcely breathed. He'd run fur, but he didn't have nobody on his back."

" I see ! " ejaculated the ranchman, smiting one doubled fist upon the other palm. " That Pete has fooled us from the start."

" Sure did," admitted Sam.

" He never mounted his horse at all? " cried Frances, deeply interested.

" That's it," said her father. " We ought to

have known that at the time.   No horse could
have gone smashing through the brush the way
that one did without knocking his rider's head off."

" Sure," agreed Sam again.

" And he was right there near the place he held
Pratt and me captive all the time we were making
a stretcher for poor Pratt," said Frances.

" Or hiking up stream," said the foreman, preparing to ride down to the corral.

" Lucky the boy broke the fellow's gun as he
did," said Captain Rugley, thoughtfully, turning
to his daughter.   " Otherwise some of us might
have been popped off from the bushes."

" Oh, Daddy ! "

" When a man's as mean as that scalawag," said
her father, philosophically, " there's no knowing
to what lengths he will go.   I shan't feel that you
are safe on the ranges until he's found and jailed."

" And I shan't feel that we're out of trouble
until your friend Mr. Lonergan comes here and
you divide and get rid of that silly old treasure,"
declared Frances, and she pouted a little.

" What's that, Frances? " gasped the old Captain.   " All those jewels and stuff?   Why, don't
you care anything for them? "

" I care more for my peace of mind," she said,
decidedly.   " And see what it's brought poor Pratt
to."

"Well," said her father, subsiding. "The boy did git the dirty end of the stick, for a fact. I'm sorry he was hurt——"

"And you are sorry you thought so ill of him, too, Daddy—you know you are," whispered Frances, one arm stealing over the Captain's shoulder.

"Well——"

"Now, "fess up!"" she laughed, softly. "He's a good boy to risk himself for me."

"I wouldn't have thought much of him if he hadn't," said the old ranchman, stubbornly.

"What could you really expect when you consider that he has lived all his life in a city——"

"And works in a bank," finished the Captain, with a sly grin. "But I reckon I have got to take off my hat to him. He's a hero."

"He is a good boy," Frances said, cheerfully. "And I hope that he will recover all right, as the doctor says he will."

"I don't know how fast he'll mend," chuckled the Captain. "If I were he, and getting the attention he is——"

"From whom?" demanded Frances, turning on him sharply.

"From Ming, of course," responded her father, soberly, but with his eyes a-twinkle.

And then Frances fled upstairs again, her cheeks

burning as she heard the old ranchman's mellow laughter.

Pratt lay on his bed with his head swathed in bandages and his shoulder in a brace. He had suffered a dislocation as well as the bruises and the cut in his head. From the time he had been struck from behind by the man, Pete, the young fellow had known nothing at all until he awoke to find himself stretched upon this bed in the Bar-T ranch-house.

The old Captain, with Ming's help, had disrobed Pratt and put him to bed; but when the doctor came early in the morning, he put the patient in Frances' hands.

" What he needs is good nursing. Don't leave him to the men," said the doctor. " Your father says he's cured himself by getting out on horseback. If it didn't kill him, I admit it's aiding in his cure for him to be more active again.

" But I depend upon you, my dear, to keep this patient as quiet as possible. I hate having my patients get away from me," added the physician with twinkling eye. "And this lad is mine for some time. He has sure been badly shaken up."

He was afraid at first that there was concussion of the brain; but after a few hours the young bank clerk became lucid in his speech and the fever began to decrease.

The doctor had not left the ranch until the evening before this day when Frances stole up the stair again to peer into the room to see how her patient was.

"Oh, I'm awake!" cried Pratt, cheerfully. "You don't expect me to sleep all the time, do you, Frances?"

"Sleep is good for you," declared the girl of the ranges, with a sober smile. "The doctor says you are to keep very quiet."

"Goodness! I might as well be buried and so save my board," grumbled Pratt. "When is he going to let me get up out of this?"

"Not for a long, long time yet," said Frances, seriously.

"What? Why, I could get up now——"

"With those shingles plastered to your shoulder?" asked the girl, smiling again, but somewhat roguishly.

"Oh—well—have those boards actually got to stay on?"

"Yes, indeed."

"How long?"

"Till the doctor removes them, Pratt. Now, be a good boy."

"I'll never be able to get out of bed," grumbled the patient, "if he keeps me here much longer. I'll be bedridden."

" Nonsense," said Frances, with a very superior
air.   " You haven't been here two days yet."

" And when is the doctor coming again? " went
on Pratt.

" He said he'd come within the week," replied
the girl, demurely.

" Good-night, nurse! " groaned Pratt.   " A
whole week?   Why, I'll die in that time—posi-
tively."

" You only think so," said Frances, coolly.

" You don't know how hard it is to lie here with
nothing to do."

" You don't appreciate your good fortune, I am
afraid," returned the girl, more gravely.   " You
might have been much more seriously hurt—— "

" You don't suppose I care about being hurt, do
you? " he cried, with some excitement.   "I'd go
through it a dozen times to the same end,
Frances—— "

" Now, stop! " she said, commandingly, and
raising an admonitory finger.   " If you show any
excitement I will go out of the room and leave
Ming—— "

" Don't! " groaned Pratt.

" I shall certainly leave him in charge of you.
You won't talk to him."

" No.   If he doesn't sit silent like a yellow
graven image, he scatters ' l's ' all about the room

until I want to get out of bed and sweep 'em up,"
declared Pratt.

The ranchman's daughter smiled at him, but
shook her head. " Now! no more talking. I'll sit
here and promise not to scatter any of the alpha-
bet broadcast; but you must keep still."

" That's mighty hard," muttered the patient.
" Sit over by the window. There! right in the sun.
I like to see your hair when the sun burnishes it."

Frances promptly removed her seat to the shady
side of the room.

" Oh, please! " begged Pratt. " I'm sick, you
know. You really ought to humor me."

" And you really ought not to jolly me! "
laughed the range girl. " I think you are a tease,
Pratt."

" Honest! I mean it."

She looked at him with a roguish smile. " What
did you say to Miss Latrop about her hair? Isn't
it a lovely blond? "

" Oh! I never looked at it twice. Molasses
color," declared Pratt. " I don't like such light
hair."

" Now, be still. Mrs. Edwards sent over word
they are coming to see you to-morrow. If you are
feverish I shan't let them in."

" My goodness! " gasped Pratt. " Not all of
them coming, I hope? "

THE OLD HACIENDA TOOK ON A LIVELINESS OF ASPECT
THAT IT HAD NEVER KNOWN BEFORE.   *Page 253.*

" Mrs. Edwards and Miss Latrop, anyway,"
said Frances, seriously. " Now keep still."

Pratt digested this for a while; then he held up
one arm and waved it.

" Well?   What is it? " asked the stern nurse.

" Please, teacher! "

" Well? "

" May I say one thing? "

" Just one.   Then silence for an hour."

" If that girl from Boston comes I'm going to
have a fever—understand?   I don't want her up
here.   Now, that's all there is about it."

" Hush, small boy!   You don't know what is
good for you.   You must leave it to the doctor and
me," said Frances, but she kept her head turned
from the bed so that Pratt would not see her eyes.

By and by Pratt waved his hand again like a
pupil in school and even snapped his fingers to
attract her attention.

" Please, teacher! " he begged when she looked
up from the pad on her knee over which her pencil
had been traveling so rapidly.

" I'm nurse, not teacher," Frances said, firmly.

" Nurse, then.   Is that the plan for the pageant
you are writing? "

" A part of it," she admitted.   " Some ideas
that came to me the time I went to Amarillo."

" With the make-believe treasure chest? "

" Yes."

" Read it to me, will you, Miss Nurse? " he asked.

" If you will keep still.   I never did see such a chatterbox! " exclaimed Frances, in vexation.

" I'll be just as still as still! " he promised. " Maybe it will put me to sleep."

" Mercy! I hope it isn't as dull as all that," she said, and began to read the pages she had written.

CHAPTER XXVII

THE girl from Boston did not come over to see Pratt that very next day; but soon she, as well as the remainder of the young people who had been the guests of Mr. Bill Edwards and his hospitable wife, were stopping at the Bar-T daily and inquiring for Pratt; and as soon as he could be helped downstairs and out upon the veranda, he held a general reception all day long.

In the afternoon when the Edwards crowd was over, the old *hacienda* took on a liveliness of aspect that it had never known before. The veranda was gay with bright frocks and the air resounded with laughter.

The boys gathered around Pratt and plans for future hunts and other junkets were made—for the young bank clerk was rapidly recovering. The girls meanwhile made much of the old Captain— all but Sue Latrop. But she did not count for as much as she had at the beginning of her visit at the Edwards ranch. The other young folk had begun to find her out.

The punchers who were off duty were attracted

to this gay party on the porch, as naturally as flies gravitate to molasses. The Amarillo girls—and, of course, Mrs. Bill Edwards—saw nothing out of the way in Captain Rugley's hands lounging up to the *hacienda* to talk. Most of them were young fellows of neighboring families, and quite as well known as were the visitors themselves. Sue Latrop's amazement at this familiarity only made the other girls laugh.

Unless she would be left alone on the veranda with Pratt (which she considered very bad form) she was obliged one afternoon to go down to the corral with the crowd to see a bunch of ponies fresh from the range.

Some of the half-wild ponies rolled their eyes, snorted, and galloped to the far side of the corral the instant the visitors appeared.

"Get your reserved seats, gals!" cried Fred Purchase, preparing to open the gate. "Roost all along the rail up there and watch the fun. I bet Fatty Obendorf falls off and breaks a suspender-button—fust throw out of the box!"

"Oh my! you don't mean for us to climb up *there?*" gasped Sue, as one or two of her friends tucked up their skirts and started to mount the fence.

"Sure. Reserved seats at the top," laughed Mrs. Edwards, likewise mounting the barrier.

"Why! I am afraid I could never do it," murmured the Boston girl.

"You'll miss a lot of fun, then," declared one of the Amarillo girls, callously. They were all getting a little tired of Sue Latrop and her pose.

Finding herself the only one on the ground, Sue scrambled up very clumsily and just in time to see Fatty rope the first pony out of the bunch that was now racing around and around the corral.

This was a black and white rascal with a high head and rolling eye, that looked as though he had never been bridled in his life. But it was only that he had been some months on the range, and freedom had gone to his head.

Fatty lay back on the lariat and dug his high heels into the sod. When the pony felt the noose he leaped into it, it tightened around his neck, and the creature came to the ground, kicking and squealing.

"By hicketty!" yelled Purchase. "Ain't lil' old Fatty good for suthin'? Yuh could suah use him tuh tie a steamboat tuh—what!"

For all the fun the other punchers made of Fatty Obendorf, he had his selection out of the herd blindfolded, bridled, and saddled, before any other pony was noosed.

"Good for you, Fatty!" cried Frances, who was perched on the corral fence with the other girls. " And that's a good horse, too; only you want to 'ware heels. I remember that he's a kicker."

" Oh! Fatty don't keer if his fust name's Kickapoo," jeered Fred.

The black and white pony gave Obendorf all the work he wanted for some minutes, however, and afforded the spectators much excitement. He wasn't a bucking bronco, but he showed plainly his dislike for human management. Spur and bit and quirt, however, was a combination that the pony was quickly forced to give in to.

Fred himself straddled a speckled, ugly-looking animal, and put it through its paces in short order. It was a spectacular exhibition; but some of the other punchers laughed uproariously.

" What's the matter with you fellers, anyway? " demanded Fred, complainingly. " Ain't you a-gwine to accord me no praise? Don't I look as purty on hawseback as that fat chunk does? " he added, referring to Obendorf.

" You know very well," called Frances, from the seat of judgment, " that I drove that speckled pony to my little jumpcart two years ago. That's Chippy—and he's almost as big a bluff, Fred, as you are! He looks savage enough to eat you up, and is really as tame as tame can be."

" Hi, Teddie! she's got yuh throwed, tied, an'

branded, all right!" shouted one of the other punchers.

The girls on the fence welcomed each feat of horsemanship with great applause. Some of the ponies "acted up," as Tom Gallup called it, "to the queen's taste."

"Whatever that may mean, Tom," Mrs. Edwards said, dryly. "Why don't you try your 'prentice hand on that buckskin? He's dodged the lariat a dozen times."

"Why, that Bucky is a regular rocking-horse, I bet," declared Tom, who, for a city boy, was a pretty good rider.

"Get down and ride him, Tommy," urged Sue. "Can't you ride as well as these country boys?"

"I never said I could," retorted Tom, doubtfully. "You girls are guying the punchers, too. Why don't one o' you get down and show 'em what you can do?"

"Frances can beat all you boys riding, Tommy," Mrs. Edwards cried.

"Bet she couldn't even get aboard of that Bucky," young Gallup instantly responded.

"You're not going to take a dare like that, are you, Frances?" demanded Mrs. Edwards.

Sue became disdainful the moment Frances came into the argument. She had nothing further to say.

"I believe the boys are all holding back on that little buckskin," said Frances, laughing.

"Step right this way, Ma'am, step right this way," urged Fred Purchase, bowing low and offering his lariat. "Here's my rope and I'll lend ye anything else ye may need if ye wanter try that Bucky. He's some bronco, believe me!"

Frances got down off the fence.

"Oh! don't you try it, Frances!" cried one nervous girl. "That pony looks wicked!"

"Let her break her neck, if she wants to make a fool of herself!" snapped Sue, *sotto voce*.

Nobody heard her. All were watching too closely the range girl approach the buckskin pony. She had accepted Fred's lariat and the coil of it began to whirl about her head.

"There it goes!" cried Tom Gallup.

The buckskin started on a long, swinging lope; but it could not get out from under the coil of the lariat. The noose fell and the plunging pony went head and forefeet into it. Frances leaped with both feet upon the rope, just as it snapped taut. Bucky went on his head, kicking all four feet in the air.

"Got him! got him!" shrieked the excited Tom, and the girls cheered likewise.

And then the lariat snapped in two!

Muddied and scratched, the buckskin scrambled

to his feet, his eyes blazing, nostrils distended, and as wild a horse as ever came off the range.

"Look out, Miss Frances!" yelled Mack Hinkman, who had just come upon the scene. "That thar buckskin hawse is a bad actor."

"Oh! the dear girl! Whatever did possess me to urge her on?" cried Mrs. Edwards. "Boys! Save her!"

But it was all over before any of the punchers, or the visitors on the fence, could go to Frances' rescue.

The buckskin rose on his hind legs and struck at the girl desperately. She had gathered in the slack of the broken lariat and she swung it sharply across the pony's face, leaping sideways to avoid him.

The pony whirled and struck again, whistling shrilly, the foam flying from his jaws. Once more Frances avoided him.

Tom Gallup was yelling like a wild boy on the fence. Sue could scarcely catch her breath for fear. She would not have admitted it for the world; but the courage of the range girl amazed her. Her own rescue from the charge of the little black bullock by Frances had not impressed Sue Latrop as did this battle with the pony in the arena of the horse corral.

Fred Purchase ran with another lariat. Frances

seized it, flung the noose over the upraised head of the pony, took a swift turn around a shed post, and brought the " bad actor " up short.

She insisted, too, on cinching on the saddle and putting the bit in the pony's mouth.   Then she mounted him and as he tore around the corral, the girl sitting as though she were a part of the creature, the boys and girls joined the punchers in cheering her.

It was not in this way, however, that the girl visitors to the ranges learned the true worth of Frances Rugley. They were, after all, only " porch acquaintances."   Once only had the party been invited into the inner court for luncheon, and their brief calls to the ranch-house offered little opportunity for the girls to really see Frances' home.

They had met her so much in riding costume that, like Pratt Sanderson, they were amazed when she appeared in a pretty house dress. And they were really a bit awed by her, for although the range girl was of a naturally cheerful disposition, she possessed, too, more than her share of dignity.

" You don't flit about like these other girls, Frances," said the old ranchman, who was very observant.   " You grow to look and seem more like your mother every day. But the goodness knows I don't want you to grow into a woman ahead of your time."

" I reckon I won't do that, Dad," she said, laughing at him fondly.

" I don't know. I reckon you've had too much responsibility on those shoulders of yours. You left school too young, too. That's what these other girls say. Why, that Boston girl is going to school now!

" But, shucks! she wouldn't know enough to hurt her if she attended school from now till the end of time! "

Frances laughed again. " That is pretty harsh, father. Now, I think I have had quite schooling enough to get along. I don't need the higher branches of education to help you run this ranch. Do I? "

" By mighty! " exploded the Captain. " I don't know whether I have been doing right by you or not. I've been talking to Mrs. Bill Edwards about it. I loved you so, Frances, that I hated to have you out of my sight. But—— "

" Now, now! " cried the girl. " Let's have no more of that. You and I have only each other, and I couldn't bear to be away from you long enough to go to a boarding school."

" Yes—I know," went on Captain Rugley.

" But there are ways of getting around *that*. We'll see."

One thing he was determined on was Captain Dan Rugley. He proposed to have " some doings " at the ranch-house before Pratt was well enough to be discharged from " St. Frances' Hospital," as he called the *hacienda*.

The old ranchman worked up the idea with Mrs. Edwards before Frances knew anything about it.

" They call it a ' dinner dance,' " he confided to Frances at length, when the main plan was already made. " At least that's what Mrs. Edwards says."

" A ' dinner dance '? " repeated his daughter, not sure for the moment that she wished to have so much confusion in the house when there was so much to do.

" Yes ! Now, it isn't one of those dances you read about out East, where folks drink a cup of tea, and then get up and dance around, and then take a sandwich and the orchestra strikes up another tune," chuckled Captain Rugley.

" No, it isn't like that. I couldn't stand any such doings. I'd never know when I'd had enough to eat; every dance would shake down the courses so that my stomach would be packed as hard as a cement sidewalk."

"Oh, Daddy!" said Frances, half laughing at him.

"No. This dinner dance idea is all right," declared the ranchman. "We give a dinner to the whole crowd—all the girls and boys that have been coming over here for the past two or three weeks."

"It will make fifteen at table," said the practical Frances, thinking hard of the resources of the household.

"That's all right. I'll get in the Reposa boys to help San Soo and Ming."

"Victorino, too?" asked his daughter, curiously.

"Yes," declared the Captain, stoutly. "He's sorry he mixed up with Ratty M'Gill. Vic isn't a bad boy. Well, that's help enough, and San Soo can outdo himself on his dinner."

"That part of it will be all right—and the service, too, for José and Victorino are handy boys," admitted Frances.

"We'll have out the best tableware we own. That silver stuff that came from Don Morales will knock their eyes out——"

"Oh, Daddy!" cried Frances, going off into a gale of laughter. "You picked up that expression from Tom Gallup."

"That's the slangy boy—yes," admitted the old

ranchman, with a broad smile. " But some of his slang just hits things off right. Some of those girls think you're ' country,' I know. We'll show them! "

Frances sighed. She knew it meant that she must dress the part of a barbarian princess to please her father. But she made no objection. If she tried to show him that the jewels and ornaments were not fit for her to wear, he would be hurt.

" Yes! " exclaimed Captain Rugley, evidently much pleased with the idea of a social time that he had evolved with Mrs. Edwards' help, " we'll have as nice a dinner as San Soo can make. After dinner we'll have dancing, I'll get the string band from Jackleg. Jackleg's getting to be quite a social centre, Mrs. Edwards says."

Frances laughed again. " I expect," she said, " that Mrs. Edwards is eager to have a dance, and the Jackleg string band *is* a whole lot better than Bob Jones' accordion and Perry's old fiddle."

" Oh, well! Of course, an accordion and fiddle are all right for a cowboy dance, but this is going to be the real thing! " declared her father.

" Aren't you going to invite the boys as usual? " asked Frances, quickly.

" Not to the dinner! " gasped her father. " But that's all right. To the dance, afterward. Some of them are mighty good dancers, and there aren't boys enough in Mrs. Edwards' crowd to go round. It's quite the thing at a dinner dance, she says, to invite extra people to come in after the dinner is over."

" All right," said Frances, suppressing another sigh.

" And I'm going to send off for half a carload of potted palms, and other plants. We'll decorate like the Town Hall. You'll see!" exclaimed the old ranchman, as eager as a boy about it all.

Frances hadn't the heart to make any objection, but she was afraid that the affair would be a disappointment to him. She did not think the boys from the ranges, and Sue Latrop and her girl friends, would mix well.

But the Captain went ahead with his preparations with his usual energy. He had Mrs. Edwards as chief adviser. But Frances overlooked the plans in the household in her usually capable way.

The big drawing-room was thoroughly cleaned and the floor waxed. The scratches made by Ratty M'Gill's spurs were eliminated. When the potted plants came—a four-mule wagon-load— Frances arranged them about the dancing floor and dining-room.

She found her father practising his steps in the

hall one morning before breakfast. " Goodness, Daddy," she cried. " Do be careful of your weak leg."

" Don't you worry about me," he chuckled. " I'm going to give old Mr. Rheumatism a black eye this time. I'm going to ' shake a leg ' at this dance if it's the last act of my life."

" Don't be too reckless," she told him, with a worried little frown on her brow. " I want you to be able to ride to Jackleg to see the pageant. And that comes the very day but one after our dance."

" I'll be all right," he assured her. " I have a dance promised from Mrs. Edwards and each of the girls but that Boston one, right now. And I wouldn't miss your show in Jackleg, Frances, for a penny!

" I only wish Lon were here to enjoy it. I got a letter from that minister saying that Lon and he will reach here next week. If they'd come early in the week they'd get here in time for the pageant, anyway."

With so much bustle and preparation about the Bar-T ranch-house, there was not much likelihood of anybody being reckless enough to attempt stealing the old Spanish chest, or its contents.

These days the Captain kept the room in which the chest of treasure lay double-locked, and at night slept in the room himself. From sunset to sunrise a relay of cowboys rode around the huge house and compound, and although Pete Marin, as Ratty M'Gill's friend from Mississippi was called, was still at large, there was no fear that he, or anybody else, would get into the *hacienda* at night.

Frances, with all her duties, had less time to devote to Pratt's entertainment now. In truth, as soon as he was able to get downstairs by himself he complained that he lost his nurse.

When the crowd came over from the Edwards ranch, and sat around on the porch, Frances was not always with them. One afternoon—the very day before the dinner and dance, in fact—she came through one of the long, open windows upon the veranda, right behind a group of three of the girls. It was by chance she heard one of them say:

" Well, I don't care, Sue, I think she is real nice. You are awfully critical."

" I can't bear dowdy people," drawled Sue Latrop. " I know she'll be a sight at that dinner to-morrow night. My goodness! if for nothing else I'd come to see how she looks in her ' best bib and tucker ' and how that queer old man acts when he is what he calls ' all dolled up.' "

. " Sh! " warned the third girl. " Somebody will hear you."

" Pooh! If they do?" returned Sue Latrop, carelessly.

" If I were you," said the other girl, with warmth, " I wouldn't accept an invitation to dine with people whom I expected to make fun of."

" Silly!" laughed the girl from Boston. " I've got to find enjoyment somewhere—and there's little enough of it in this Panhandle. I'll be glad when father writes saying that I can come home once again."

" How about your going to this dance, Sue?" chuckled one of the girls, suddenly. " I thought your doctor had forbidden dancing for this summer?"

" I think I see myself dancing with these cowboys that they are going to invite," scoffed Sue. " And Pratt can't dance yet. There isn't anybody worth dancing with in our crowd now."

" Hasn't the Captain asked you for a dance?" queried her friend, roguishly.

" I should say not!" gasped Sue. " Fancy!"

" You must not act as though his invitation insulted you, Sue Latrop," said one of the other girls, rather tartly. " You might as well understand, first as last, that we are all fond of Captain Rugley. Besides, he's a very influential man and one of the wealthiest in this part of the Panhandle."

"*Nouveau-riche*," sniffed Miss Sue, with a toss of her head.

"If that means newly rich, why, he's not!" exclaimed the other girl, with continued warmth. "It's true, he didn't make his money baking beans, or bean-pots; nor by drying and selling pollock and calling it ' codfish.' I believe one has to make his money in some such way to break into Boston society?"

"Something like that," responded Sue, calmly.

"Well, the old Captain is very, very wealthy," went on his champion. "If you'd ever been much inside this big house, you'd see it is so. And they say he has a treasure chest containing jewels of fabulous value."

"A treasure chest!" ejaculated the Boston girl.

"Yes, Ma'am!"

"Now you are trying to fool me," declared Sue Latrop.

"You wait! I expect Frances will wear at the dinner some of those wonderful old jewels the Captain digs out of his chest once in a while. I've heard they are really amazing——"

"Jewels to deck out the Cattle Queen!" interrupted Sue, tauntingly. "Nose ring and anklets included, I s'pose?"

"Now, Sue! how can you be so mean?" cried one of the other girls.

" Pshaw! I suppose she'll be a wondrous sight in her ' best bib and tucker.' Loaded down with silver ornaments, like a Mexican belle at a fair, or an Indian squaw at a poodle-dog feast. She will undoubtedly throw all us girls in the shade," and Sue burst into a gale of laughter.

"I declare! you're cruel, Sue!" cried one of the girls from Amarillo.

"I'd like to know how you make that out, Miss?" demanded the girl from Boston.

"Frances has never done you a bit of harm. Why! you are accepting her hospitality this very moment. And yet, you haven't a good word to say for her."

" I don't see that I am called upon to give her a good word," sneered Miss Latrop. "She is a rough, rude, quite impossible person. I fail to see wherein she deserves any consideration at my hands. I declare! to hear you girls, one would think this cowgirl was of some importance."

Frances came quietly away from the window, postponing her dusting in that quarter until later. But she was tempted—very sorely tempted indeed.

Sue expected her to look like a cross between an Indian squaw and a Mexican belle at dinner—and Frances was sorely tempted to fulfil the Boston girl's idea of what a " cattle queen " should look like at a society function!

CHAPTER XXVIII

THE BURSTING OF THE CHRYSALIS

Frances Durham Rugley was growing up. At least, she felt a great many years older now than she did that day so short a time before when, riding along the trail, she had heard Pratt and the mountain lion fighting in Brother's Coulie.

She looked at her reflection in the long dressing-mirror in her own room, and could not see that she had added to her stature in this time " one jot or tittle." But inside she felt worlds older.

It was the afternoon of the dinner-party day. She had come upstairs to make ready to receive her guests. The dinner was for seven and Frances had given herself plenty of time to dress.

Pratt was off on his pony, " getting the stiffness out of himself," he declared. The old Captain was just as busy as a bee, and just as fussy as a clucking hen, about the last preparations for the party.

And meanwhile Frances was undecided. She almost wished she might run away from the ordeal before her. To face all these people whom, after all, she knew so slightly, and play hostess at her

father's table, and be criticised by them all, was an
ordeal hard for the range girl to face.

She was not particularly shy; but she shrank
from unkind remarks, and she was sure of having
at least one critic-extraordinary at the table—Sue
Latrop.

This was really Frances' " coming out party "¡
but she didn't want to " come out " at all!

" Oh! I wish they had never come here.   I wish
daddy had not asked them to this dinner.   Dear
me!" groaned the girl of the ranges, " I almost
wish I had never met Pratt at all."

For, looking into the future, she saw a long
vista of range work and quiet living, with merely
the minor incidents of ranch life to break the
monotony.   This " dip " into society would not
even leave a pleasant remembrance, she was
afraid.

And it might be years before she would be
called upon to play hostess in such a way as this
again.   She sighed and unbraided her hair.   At
that moment there sounded a knock upon her
door.

She ran to open it to her father.

" Here you are, Frances," said the old ranchman, jovially.   " Never mind if Lon hasn't got
here yet; I've gone deeper into the treasure chest.
I want you to be all dolled up to-night."

His hands were fairly ablaze—or looked to be. He had his great palms cupped, and that cup was full of gems in all sorts of ancient settings—shooting sparks of all colors in the dimly lighted room.

" There's a handful of stuff to make you pretty," he said, proudly.

The ancient belt dangled over his arm. He placed all the things on her dressing-table, and stood off to admire their brilliancy. Frances swallowed a lump in her throat. How could she disappoint him! How could she try to tell him how unsuitable these gems were for a young girl in her teens! He would be heart-broken if she did not wear them.

" You are a dear, Daddy! " she murmured, and kissed him. " Now run away and let me dress."

He tiptoed out, all a-smile. His wife's dressing-room had been a " holy of holies " to this simple-minded old man, and Frances reminded him every day, more and more strongly, of the woman whom he had worshiped for a few happy years.

Frances did not hasten with her preparations, however. She sat down and spread the gewgaws out before her on the dresser. The belt, Spanish earrings of fabulous value and length, rings that almost blinded her when she held the stones in the sunlight, a great oval brooch, bracelets, and a necklace of matched stones that made her heart beat almost to suffocation when she tried it on her brown throat.

She had it in her power to "knock their eyes out," as daddy (and Tom Gallup) had expressed it. She could bedeck herself like a queen. She knew that Sue Latrop worshiped the tangible signs of wealth, as she understood them.

Cattle, and range lands, and horses, and a great, rambling house like this at the Bar-T, impressed the girl from Boston very little. But jewels would appeal to her empty head as nothing else could.

Frances knew this very well. She knew that she could overawe the Boston girl with a display of these gems. And she would please her father, too, in loading her fingers and ears and neck and arms with the brilliants.

And then, before she got any farther in her dressing, or had decided in her troubled mind what really to do, there came another, and lighter, tapping on her door.

"Who's there?" asked Frances.

"It's only me, Frances," said Pratt.

"What do you want?" she asked, calmly, rising and approaching the door.

"Got something for you—if you want them," the young man said, in a low voice.

"What is it?" she queried.

"Open the door and see," and he laughed a little nervously.

Frances drew her gown closer about her throat, and turned the knob. Instantly a great bunch of fragrant little blossoms—the wild-flowers so hard to find on the plains and in the foothills—were thrust into her hands.

"Oh, *Pratt!*" shrieked the girl in delight.

She clasped the blossoms to her bosom; she buried her face in them. Pratt watched her with smiling lips, and wonderingly.

How pretty and girlish she was! The grown-up air that responsibilities had lent her fell away like a cloak. She was just a simple, enthusiastic, delighted girl, after all!

"Like them?" asked the young man, laconically.

"I *love* them!" Frances declared.

Pratt was thinking how wonderful it was that a girl could seize a big bunch of posies like that, and hug them, and press them to her face, and still not crush the fragile things.

"Why," he thought, "I've had to handle them like eggs all the way here, to keep from spoiling them beyond repair. Aren't girls wonders?"

You see, Pratt Sanderson was beginning to be interested in the mysteries of the opposite sex.

"Run away now, like a good boy," she said to

him, as she had to her father, and closed the door once more.

She ran to her bathroom and filled two vases with water and put the flower stems in, that they might drink and keep the blossoms fresh.

Then, with a lighter air and tread, she went about her dressing for the party.

She put up her hair, deftly copying the fashion that Sue Latrop—that mirror of Eastern fashion —affected.   And the new mode became Frances vastly.

Her new dress—the one she had had made for the pageant—had already come home from the city dressmaker who had her measurements.   She spread it upon the bed and got her skirts and other linen.

Half an hour later she was out of her bath and ready for the dress itself.   It went on and fitted perfectly.

" I am sure anybody must admire this," she told herself.   She was sure that none of the girls at the dinner and dance would be more fitly dressed than herself—if she stopped right here!

But now she returned to the dresser and looked at the blazing gems from the old Spanish chest. If only daddy did not want her to wear them!

A ring, one bracelet, possibly the brooch.   She might wear those without shocking good taste.

All were beautiful; but the heavy settings, the great belt of gold and emeralds, the necklace of sparkling brilliants—all, all were too rich and too startling for a girl of her age, and well Frances knew it.

With sinking heart and trembling fingers she adorned herself with the heaviest weight of trouble she had ever borne.

A little later she descended the stairs, slowly, regally, bearing her head erect, and looking like a little tragedy queen as she appeared in the soft evening glow at the foot of the stairs.

Pratt's gasp of wonder and amazement made the old Captain turn to look.

Above her brow was a crescent of sparkling stones. The long, graceful earrings lay lovingly upon the bared, velvet shoulders of the girl.

The bracelets clasped the firm flesh of her arms warmly. The collar of gems sparkled at her throat. The brooch blazed upon her bosom. And around her slender waist was the great belt of gold.

She was a wonderful sight! Pratt was dazzled —amazed. The old ranchman poked him in the ribs.

"What do you think of *that?*" he demanded. "Went right down to the bottom of the chest to get all that stuff. Isn't she the whole show?"

And Frances had hard work to keep back the
tears. She knew that was exactly what she was—a
show.

She could see the change slowly grow in Pratt's
features.   His wonder shifted to disapproval.
After the first shock he realized that the exhibition
of the gems on such an occasion as this was in bad
taste.

Why! she was like a jeweler's window!   The
gems were wonderfully beautiful, it was true.   But
they would better be on velvet cushions and behind
glass to be properly appreciated.

" Do you like me, Daddy? " she asked, softly.

" My mercy, Frances!   I scarcely know you,"
he admitted.   " You certainly make a great
show."

" Are you satisfied? " she asked again.

" I—I'd ought to be," he breathed, solemnly.
" You—you're a beauty!   Isn't she, Pratt? "

" Save my blushes," Frances begged, but not
lightly.   " If I suit you exactly, Daddy, I shall
appear at dinner this way."

" Sure!   Show them to our guests.   There's not
another woman in the Panhandle can make such a
show."

Frances, with a sharp pain at her heart, thought
this was probably true.

" Wait, Daddy," she said.   " Let me run back

and make one little change. You wait there in the cool reception-room, and see how I look next time."

She could no longer bear the expression of Pratt's eyes. Turning, she gathered up her skirts and scuttled back to her room. Her cheeks were afire. Her lips trembled. She had to fight back the tears.

One by one she removed the gaudy ornaments. She left the crescent in her wavy brown hair and the old-fashioned brooch at her breast. Everything else she stripped off and flung into a drawer, and locked it.

These two pieces of jewelry might be heirlooms that any young girl could wear with taste at her " coming out " party.

She ran to the vases and took a great bunch of Pratt's flowers which she carried in her gloved hand when she went down for the second time to show herself to her father.

This time she tripped lightly. Her cheeks were becomingly flushed. Her bare throat, brown and firm, rose from the soft laces of her dress in its unadorned beauty. The very dress she wore seemed more simple and girlish—but a thousand times more fitting for her wearing.

" Daddy ! "

She burst into the dimly lighted room. He

wheeled in his chair, removed the pipe from his mouth, and stared at her again.

This time there was a new light in his eyes, as there was in hers. He stood up and something caught him by the throat—or seemed to—and he swallowed hard.

" How do you like me now? " she whispered, stretching her arms out to him.

" My—my little girl! " murmured the old Captain, and his voice broke. " Then—then you are not grown up, after all? "

" Nor do I want to be, for ever and ever so long yet, Daddy! " she cried, and ran to enfold him in her warm embrace.

" Humph! " said the old Captain, confidentially. " I was half afraid of that young person who was just down here, Frances. I can kiss you now without mussing you all up, eh? "

Pratt had stolen out of the room through one of the windows to the veranda.

His heart was swelling and salt tears stung his eyes.

Like the old Captain, the youth had felt some awe of the richly-bedecked young girl who had displayed to such advantage the stunning and wonderful old jewelry that had once adorned Spanish señoras or Aztec princesses. Despite the fact that he disapproved of such a barbarous display, Pratt had been impressed.

He had an inkling, too, as to Sue Latrop's attitude toward the range girl and believed that some unkind expression of the Boston girl's feelings had tempted Frances to show herself in barbaric guise at the dinner. Pratt could not have blamed the Western girl if she had " knocked their eyes out," to use Tom Gallup's expression, with an exhibition of the gorgeous jewels Captain Rugley had got out of the treasure chest.

Without much doubt the old ranchman would have been very proud of his daughter's beauty, set off by the glitter of the wonderful old gems. It was his nature to boast of his possessions, although his pride in them was innocent enough. His wealth would never in this wide world make Captain Dan Rugley either purse-proud or arrogant!

The old man's sweetness of temper, kindliness of manner, and open-handedness had been inherited by Frances. She was a true daughter of her father. But she was her mother's child, too. The well-bred, quiet, tactful lady whom the old Border fighter had married had left her mark upon the range girl. Frances possessed natural refinement and good taste. It was that which had caused her to go to her chamber after the

display of the jewels, and return for a second
" review."

The appearance of the simply-dressed girl who
had come downstairs the second time had so
impressed Pratt Sanderson that he wished to get
off here on the porch by himself for a minute or
two.

The first load of visitors was just driving up
to the gate of the compound.

He watched the girls from Amarillo, and Sue,
and all the others descend, shake out their ruffles,
and run up the steps.

" My! " sighed Pratt Sanderson in his soul.
" Frances has got them all beat in every little way.
That's as sure as sure! "

CHAPTER XXIX

" THE PANHANDLE—PAST AND PRESENT "

JACKLEG was in holiday attire. It was a raw Western settlement, it was true; but there was more business ambition and public spirit in the place than in half a dozen Eastern towns of its population.

The schoolhouse was a long, low structure, seating as many people as the ordinary town hall. It was situated upon a flat bit of prairie on the outskirts of the town. Rather, the town had grown from the schoolhouse to the railroad station, on either side of a long, dusty street. Railroads in the West do not go out of their way to touch immature settlements. The settlements have to stretch tentacles out to the place where the railroad company determines to build a station.

This was so at Jackleg, but it gave a long vista of Main Street from the heart of the town to its outlying suburbs. This street was now gay with flags and bunting, while there were many arches of colored electric lights to burn at night.

Almost before the plans for the pageant had

been formed, the business men of Jackleg had sub-
scribed a liberal sum to defray expenses. As the
plans for the entertainment progressed, and it was
whispered about what a really fine thing it was to
be, more subscriptions rolled in.

But Captain Dan Rugley had deposited a guar-
antee with the Committee that he would pay any
debts over the subscriptions received, therefore
Frances and her helpers had gone ahead along
rather lavish lines.

The end wall of the school building had been
actually removed. The framework of the wall
was rearranged by the carpenters like the pro-
scenium arch of a stage, and a drop of canvas
faced the spectators where the teacher's desk and
platform had been.

Behind the schoolhouse was a vacant lot. This
had been surrounded with a high board fence.
The enclosure made the great stage for the spectacle which the Jackleg people, the ranchers and
farmers from around about, and the visitors from
Amarillo and other towns, had come to see.

At the back of this enclosure, or stage, was a
big sheet, or screen, on which moving pictures
could be thrown. On a platform built outside,
and over the open end of the building, were two
moving picture machines with operators who had
come on from California where some of the pic-

tures had been made by a very famous film company.

Some of the pictures had been made in Oklahoma, too, where one public-spirited American citizen has saved a herd of the almost extinct bison that once roamed our Western plains in such numbers.

At either side of the fenced yard behind the schoolhouse stood the actors in the spectacle—both human and dumb—with all the paraphernalia. A director had come on from the film company to stage the show; but the story as developed was strictly in accordance with Frances Rugley's "plans and specifications."

"She's a wonder, that little girl," declared the professional. "She'd make her mark as a scenario writer—no doubt of that. I'd like to get her for our company; but they say her father is one of the richest men in the Panhandle."

Pratt Sanderson, to whom he happened to say this, nodded. "And one of the best," he assured the Californian. "Captain Dan Rugley is a noble old man, a gentleman of the old school, and one who has seen the West grow up and develop from the times of its swaddling clothes until now."

"Wonderful country," sighed the director. "Look at its beginnings almost within the memory of the present generation, and now—why! there's half a hundred automobiles parked right outside this show to-night! "

Captain Dan Rugley secured a front seat. He was as excited as a boy over the event. He admitted to Mrs. Bill Edwards that he hadn't been to a " regular show " a dozen times in his life.

" And I expect this is going to knock the spots out of ai.ything I ever saw—even the Grand Opera at Chicago, when my wife and I went on our honeymoon."

The young folks from the Edwards ranch were scattered about the old Captain. Sue Latrop had assumed her most critical attitude. But Sue had been wonderfully silent about Frances and her father since the dinner dance.

That occasion had turned out to be something entirely different from what the girl from Boston expected. In the first place, her young hostess was better and more tastefully—though simply— dressed than any of her guests.

Her adornments had been only a crescent in her hair and a brooch; but Sue had been forced to admire the beauty and value of these. Beside Frances, the other girls seemed overdressed. The range girl had dignity enough to carry off her part perfectly.

Under the soft glow of the candles in the wonderful old candelabra, to which the Captain referred as " a part of the loot of Señor Morales' *hacienda*," Frances of the ranges sat as hostess, calmly beautiful, and governing the course of the dinner without the least hesitancy or confusion.

She looked out for every guest's needs and directed the two Mexican boys and Ming in their service with all the calmness and judgment of a hostess who was long used to dinner parties. Indeed, Sue Latrop was forced to admit in her secret soul that she had never seen any hostess manage better at an entertainment of this kind.

At the upper end of the table, the old Captain fairly beamed his hospitality and delight. He kept the boys in a gale of laughter, and the girls seemed all to enjoy themselves, too. Critical Miss Latrop could throw no wet blanket upon the proceedings; to tell the truth, her sour face was quite overlooked by the other guests, and about all the attention she attracted was when Mrs Bill Edwards asked her if she had the toothache.

" No, I have no toothache! " snapped Sue. " I don't see why you should ask."

" Well, my dear," said the lady, soothingly, " something must surely be the matter. I never saw a person at dinner with so miserable a countenance. Does something pinch you? "

Yes! it was Sue's vanity pinching her, if the truth were known. Her diatribes about Frances

and the old Captain were not to be easily forgotten by the girl from Boston.   Not so much was
she smitten because of her unkindness; but she felt
that she had played the fool!

Her friends from Amarillo must be quietly
laughing in secret over what Sue had said regarding the uncouthness of the Captain and the lack
of breeding of the " Cattle Queen."   Sue felt that
she had laid herself open to ridicule, and it did
hurt Sue Latrop to think that her young friends
were laughing at her.

As for the dinner, that was a revelation to the
girl from Boston.   The service, if a bit odd, was
very good.   And the silver, cut glass, napery, and
all were as rich as Sue had ever seen.

After the dinner, and the other guests began to
arrive, and the band struck up behind the palms in
the inner court of the *hacienda,* Sue continued to
be surprised, though she failed to admit it to her
friends.

It was true the boys came up from the bunk-
house without evening dress.   But their black
clothes were clean and well brushed, and those who
wore the usual kerchief about their necks sported
silk ones and carried their bullion-loaded som-
breros in their hands.

And they could all dance.   Sue refused the first
few dances and tried to sit and look on in a supe-

rior way; but she presently failed to make good at this.

When the kindly old ranchman considered her a wall-flower and came and begged her to " give him a whirl," Sue had to break through her "icy reserve."

Although they did not dance the more modern dances, she found that Captain Rugley knew his steps and was as light on his feet as a man half his age.

" I have given Mr. Rheumatism the time of his life to-night! " declared the owner of the Bar-T brand. " That's what I told Frances I would do."

And Captain Rugley suffered no ill effects from the dance, as was shown by his appearance here at the Jackleg schoolhouse to-night, when the canvas curtain slowly rolled up to reveal first the painted curtain behind it, on which was a picture of the meeting of Cortez and the Aztec princes soon after the Conqueror's arrival in Mexico.

The school teacher read the prologue, and the spectators settled down to listen and to see. His explanation of what was to follow was both concise and well written, and the whisper went around:

" And she's only a girl! Yes, Miss Rugley wrote it all."

Sue sniffed. The teacher stepped back into the shadow and the painted curtain rolled up.

There was a gasp of amazement when the audience saw what was revealed behind the painted sheet. One of the moving picture machines was already running, and on the great screen was thrown a representation of the staked plains of the Panhandle as they were in the days before the white man ever saw them.

Far, far away appeared a band of painted and feather-bedecked Indians, riding their mustangs, and sweeping down toward the immediate foreground of the picture with a vividness that was almost startling.

Into that foreground was drifting a herd of buffaloes. They started, the bulls giving the signal as the enemy approached, and the end of that section was the scampering of the great, hairy beasts, with the Indians in full chase, brandishing their spears.

Immediately the scene changed and a train of a different kind broke into view in the dim perspective. The moving figures grew clearer as the moments passed. Over a similar part of the staked plain came the exploring Spaniards, with their cattle and caparisoned horses, their enslaved Aztecs, their priests bearing the Cross before.

The moving procession came closer and closer until suddenly the whirring of the picture machine stopped, a great searchlight was turned upon the dusky yard between the screen and the open end of the school building, and with a gasp of amazement the audience saw there the double of the procession which had just been pictured on the moving picture screen.

The actors in this part of the pageant crowded across the desert, were stopped by a stampede of Indian ponies, and later made friends of the wondering savages.

From this point on the history of the Panhandle developed rapidly. The spectators saw the crossing of the plains by the early pioneers, both in picture and by actual people, a train of prairie schooners drawn by oxen, and a sham battle between the pioneers and the Indians.

The buffaloes disappeared from the picture and the wide-horned cattle took their place. A picture of a famous round-up was shown, and then a real herd of cattle was driven into the enclosure (they wore the Bar-T brand) and several cowboys displayed their skill in roping and tying.

The curtain was dropped, there was a swift change, and it arose again on a hastily-built frontier town—a town of one-story shacks with two-story false fronts, dance and gambling halls, saloons, a pitiful hotel, and all the crude and ugly building expressions of a raw civilization.

"My mighty!" gasped Captain Dan Rugley. "That's Amarillo—Amarillo as I first saw it, twenty-five years ago."

People appeared in the street, and rough enough they were. A band of cowpunchers rode in, with yells and pistol shots. The rough life of that early day was displayed in some detail.

And then, after a short intermission, pictures' were displayed again of great droves of cattle on the trail, bound for the shipping points; following which came pictures of the new wheat fields—that march of the agricultural régime that is to make the Panhandle one of the wealthiest sections of our great country.

A great reaper was shown at work; likewise a traction gang-plow and a motor threshing machine. The progress in agriculture in the Panhandle during the last half dozen years really excited some of the older residents.

"Did you ever see the beat of that?" demanded Captain Rugley. "I'm blest if I wouldn't like to own one of them. See those little dinguses turn up the ribbons of sod! I don't know but that Frances can encourage me to be that kind of a farmer, after all! There's something big about riding a reaper like that one. And that threshing machine, too! Did you see the straw blowing out of the pipes as though a cyclone was whirling it away?

" By mighty! I wish Lon could have been here to see this, I certainly do! "

For the last time the curtain was lowered and then rose again. On the screen was pictured Ama-rillo as it is to-day.

First a panorama of the town and its outskirts. Then "stills" of its principal buildings, and its principal citizens.

Then the main streets, full of business life, autos chugging, electric cars clanging back and forth, all of the bustle of a modern town that is growing rich and growing rapidly.

The contrast between what the spectators had seen early in the spectacle and this final scene made them thoughtful. There had been plenty of applause all through the show; but when " Good-night " was shown upon the screen, nobody moved, and Pratt raised the shout for:

" Miss Rugley! "

She would not appear before the curtain save with the other members of the committee. But the cheering was for her and she had to run away to hide her blushes and her tears of happiness.

" Wake up, Sue, it's over! " exclaimed one of the other girls, shaking the young lady from Boston.

Sue Latrop came to herself slowly. She had never realized the Spirit of the West before, nor appreciated what it meant to have battled for and grown up with a frontier community.

" Is—is that all true? " she whispered to Pratt.

" Is what all true? " he asked, rather blankly.

" That there have been such improvements and changes here in so few years? "

" You bet! " exclaimed Pratt, with emphasis.

" Well—re'lly—it's quite wonderful," admitted Sue, slowly. " I had no idea it was like that! "

" So you think better of our ' crude civilization,' do you? " laughed one of her girl friends.

" Why—why, it is quite surprising," said Sue, again, and still quite breathless.

" And what do you think of our Frances? " demanded Mrs. Bill Edwards, proudly. " There's nobody in Boston's Back Bay, even, who could do better than she? "

And Sue Latrop was—for the time being, at least—completely silenced.

CHAPTER XXX

A REUNION

THERE had been a delay on the railroad caused by a washout; therefore Jonas Lonergan and Mr. Decimus Tooley, the chaplain of the Bylittle Soldiers' Home, did not arrive at Jackleg in time for the night of the spectacle of the Pageant of the Panhandle.

But the party from the Bar-T Ranch, after the show was over and Frances and the Captain had both been congratulated, rode down to the station to meet the belated train to which was attached the special car Captain Rugley had engaged for the service of his old partner and the minister.

With the Bar-T party was Pratt, although he proposed going back to the Edwards ranch that night. He wanted to get away from the crowd of enthusiastic and excited young people who had accompanied Mr. and Mrs. Bill Edwards into town to the show.

This train that was stopping to cast loose the special car at Jackleg was the last to stop at that station at night. Some few of the spectators of the pageant would board it for stations farther west; so there was a small group on the station platform.

The young folk, Pratt and Frances, sighted the headlight up the track. They were walking up and down the platform, arm in arm and talking over the successful completion of the play, when they spied it.

"It's coming, Daddy!" cried Frances, running into the station to warn the old Captain.

To tell the truth, he had been leaning back against the wall—in a hard and straight-backed chair, of course—taking a "cat-nap." But he awoke instantly and with all his senses alert.

"All right, Frances—all right, my girl," he said. "I'm with you. Hurrah! My old partner will be as glad to see me as I am to see him."

But when the train rolled in there was some delay. The special car had to be shunted onto the siding before Captain Rugley could go aboard.

"Come on, Frances," urged her father, as eager as a boy. He ran across the tracks and Frances dutifully followed him. Pratt remained on the platform and looked rather wistfully after her. Their conversation had been broken off abruptly. He had not had an opportunity to say all that he wanted to say and he was to go back to Amarillo the next day.

He saw the Captain and his daughter climb the

steps, helped by the negro porter. They disappeared within the lighted car. Pratt still lingered. His pony was hitched up the street a block or so. There really was nothing further for him to wait for.

Suddenly shadows appeared on a curtain of one section of the car. The shade flew up and the window was raised.

The young man from Amarillo stood right where the lamplight fell upon his features. He found himself staring into the face of a grey-visaged, sharp-eyed old man, who had a great shock of grey hair on the top of his head like a cockatoo's tuft.

The stranger stared at Pratt earnestly, and then beckoned him with both hands, shouting:

" Hey, you boy! You there, with the plaid cap. Come here! "

Rather startled, and not a little amused, Pratt started slowly in the direction of the car.

" Hey! Lift your feet there," called out the old man. " You act like you had the hookworm. Git a move on! "

" What do you want? " demanded Pratt, coming under the window. He could see into the lighted car now, and he observed Frances and her father standing back of the stranger, the Captain broadly agrin.

The man reached down suddenly and grabbed Pratt by the lobe of his right ear—pinching it between thumb and finger.

" Say! what are you about? " demanded Pratt. But for a very good reason he did not seek to pull away.

" Let me look at you again," commanded the man who had taken this liberty. " Turn your face up this way—you hear me? My soul! I knew I couldn't be mistaken. What did you say this boy's name was, Dan? " he shot at the Captain over his shoulder.

" That's Pratt Sanderson," chuckled Captain Rugley. " Something of a tenderfoot, but a good lad, Lon, a good lad."

" You bet he is! " declared Jonas P. Lonergan, vigorously. " I knew his name when you spoke it, and now I know his face. He's the image of his mother—that's what he is."

Then he turned to Pratt again and roared: " Do you know who I am, boy? "

" I fancy you are the—the old partner of Captain Rugley whom he has expected so long," Pratt said, puzzled but smiling. He had never chanced to hear the expected guest called by any other name than " Lon."

" I'm Jonas P. Lonergan! " exclaimed the old man. " *Now* do you know me. I'm your mother's half-brother. I knew you folks lived out this way somewhere, but I've not seen you since you were a little shaver.

"But I'll never forget how my little half-sister used to look, and you are just like her when she was young," declared Mr. Lonergan. "Come in here, you young rascal, and let me get a closer look at you."

"My Uncle Jonas?" gasped Pratt, in amazement.

"That's what I am!" declared Mr. Lonergan. "Your old uncle who never did much of anything for you—or the rest of the fam'ly—all his life. But he's goin' to be able to do something now.

"Listen here: Captain Dan Rugley says the treasure chest old Señor Morales gave us so long ago is all right. It's chock-full of jewels and gold and money—— Shucks! I'm as crazy as a child about it," laughed the old man.

"After bein' through what I have, and livin' poor so many years, it's enough to scatter the brains of an old man like me to come into a fortune. Yes, sir! And what's mine is yours, Pratt. They tell me you are a mighty good boy. Captain Dan speaks well of you——"

"And I ought to," growled the old ranchman from the background. "I owe something to him, too, for what he did for Frances."

"Heh?" exclaimed Lonergan. He turned short around and stared at the blushing Frances. "She's a mighty fine girl, I reckon?"

"The best in the Panhandle," declared the old ranchman, nodding understandingly.

"And this boy of my sister's is a pretty good fellow, Dan?" asked Lonergan.

"Mighty fine—mighty fine," admitted Captain Dan Rugley.

"I tell you what," whispered Jonas, in the Captain's ear, "this dividin' up the contents of that old treasure chest will only be temporary after all— just temporary, eh?"

"We'll see—we'll see, Lon," said Captain Dan, carefully. "They're young yet, they're over-young. But 'twould certain sure be a romantic outcome of all our adventures together years ago, eh?"

"Right you are, Captain, right you are!" agreed Lonergan.

Frances and Pratt heard none of this. Pratt had entered the car and the two young people were talking to the Reverend Mr. Tooley, who was a demure little man in clerical black, who seemed quite happy over the reunion of the two old friends, Captain Dan Rugley and Jonas P. Lonergan.

Lonergan was a lean old man who walked with

a crutch. Although he had a very vigorous voice, he showed his age and his state of ill health when he began to move about.

"But we'll fix all that, Lon," the Captain assured him. "Once we get you out to the Bar-T we'll build you up in a jiffy. We'll get you out of doors. Humph! soldiers' home, indeed! Why, you've got a long stretch of life ahead of you yet. I've beat out old Mr. Rheumatism myself these last few weeks.

"We'll fight our bodily ills and old age together, Lon—just as we used to fight other enemies. Back to back and never give up or ask for quarter, eh?"

"That's the talk, Dan!" cried the other old fellow.

But Mr. Lonergan was glad to ride out to the Bar-T in the comfortably-cushioned carriage that Mack Hinkman had driven to town. The party arrived at the ranch-house—Mr. Tooley and all— after daybreak. The Captain had insisted upon Pratt's going, too.

"What?" Lonergan demanded. "*You* a bank clerk, looking out through the wires of a cage like a monkey in the Zoo we saw years ago at Kansas City?"

"That *is* a nice job for your nephew, hey, Lon?" put in the Captain.

"Drop it, boy, drop it.   You're the heir of a
rich man now—isn't that so, Captain?"

"That's so," agreed Captain Dan Rugley.
"He'd better write in to his bank and tell 'em to
excuse him indefinitely; and write to his mother to
come out here and visit a spell with her brother.
The Bar-T's big enough, I should hope—hey,
Frances?   What do you say?"

"I am sure it would be nice to have Pratt's
mother with us.   I'd be delighted to have somebody's mother in the house, Daddy," said Frances,
smiling.   "You know, you're the best father that
ever lived; but you can't be mother, too."

"It's what you've missed since you were a tiny
little girl, Frances," agreed Captain Rugley,
gravely.   "But just the same—I want 'em to
show me a girl in all this blessed Panhandle that's
a better or finer girl than my Frances.   Am I right,
Pratt?"

"You most certainly are, Captain," the young
man agreed.   "Or anywhere outside the Panhandle."

Frances smiled at him roguishly.   "Even from
Boston, Pratt?" she whispered.

But Pratt forgave her for that.

Another picture of the Bar-T ranch-house on a
late afternoon.   The slanting rays of a westering

sun lie across the floor of the main veranda. The family party idling there need no introduction save in a single particular.

A tall, well-built lady in black, and with grey hair, and who looks so much like Pratt Sanderson that the relationship between them could be seen at a glance, has the chair of honor. Mrs. Sanderson is making her first of many visits to the Bar-T.

Old Jonas P. Lonergan, his crutch beside him, is lying comfortably in another lounging chair. But he already looks much more vigorous.

Captain Dan Rugley, as ever, is tipped back against the wall in his favorite position. Frances is with her sewing at a low table, while Pratt is lying on the rug at his mother's feet.

"What's that Mr. Tooley said in his letter, Frances?" asked Pratt. "Is he sure the man who was killed on the railroad when he went home from here was a man named Pete Marin, who once was orderly at the soldiers' home?"

"Yes," said Frances, gravely. "He was walking the track, they thought. Either he was intoxicated or he did not hear the train. Poor fellow!"

"Blamed rascal!" ejaculated Jonas P. Lonergan.

"He made us some trouble—but it's over," said Pratt.

"You showed what sort of stuff you were made of, young man," said the Captain, thoughtfully, "at that very time. Maybe you've got something to thank that Pete for."

"And Ratty M'Gill?" asked Pratt, smiling.

"Poor Ratty!" said Frances again.

"He's gone down to the Pecos country," said the Captain, briskly. "Best place for him. Maybe he will know enough not to get in with such fellows as that Pete again."

"I should have been much afraid had I known what Pratt was getting into out here," Mrs. Sanderson ventured.

"Now, now, Sister! Don't try to make a mollycoddle out o' the boy," said Jonas P. Lonergan. "I tell you we're going to make a man out o' Pratt here. I've bought an interest in the Bar-T for him. He's going to take some of the work off the Captain's shoulders when we get him broke in, hey, Dan?"

"Right you are, Lon!" agreed the other old man.

Frances smiled quietly to hear them plan. She put her needle in and out of the work she was doing slowly. By and by her fingers stopped altogether and she looked away across the ranges.

She, too, was planning. She was seeing herself living in a college town the next winter, with daddy for company, while Mr. Lonergan and Pratt and his mother remained on at the Bar-T.

She saw herself graduating after a few years from some advanced school, quite the equal of Pratt in education. Meanwhile he would be learning to change the vast Bar-T ranges into wheat and milo fields, and taking up the new farming that is revolutionizing the Panhandle.

And after that—and after that——?

"How about Ming bringing us a pitcher of nice cool lemonade, eh, Frances?" said the Captain, breaking in upon her day-dream.

"All right, Daddy. I'll tell him," said Frances of the Ranges.

THE END